"Maybe it's be
Jake's blue ey

Callie's heart twisted. Jake wasn't only talking about a few days. He was also thinking about leaving for good. What she'd wanted from the beginning. Only now she wasn't sure she wanted him to go.

For Maisie's sake, of course.

He crouched beside his daughter on the rug. "Goodbye, Maisie." He cleared his throat. "Goodbye, BooWoo."

Maisie's lashes flickered, but she said nothing.

Slowly, he rose. "This is goodbye, then." He slung the strap of the duffel bag over his shoulder.

Callie followed him into the hall.

"I'll be back." He paused at the front door. "A day…" He shrugged. "No more than two."

She touched his arm. "Take care of yourself."

Jake's gaze flitted toward the living room. "Maisie won't miss me."

Callie ached to make things right between father and daughter, but she didn't know how.

"I'll miss you, Jake." She flushed. "I—I mean, the orchard won't be the same without you, Jake."

Lisa Carter and her family make their home in North Carolina. In addition to her Love Inspired novels, she writes romantic suspense for Abingdon Press. When she isn't writing, Lisa enjoys traveling to romantic locales, teaching writing workshops and researching her next exotic adventure. She has strong opinions on barbecue and ACC basketball. She loves to hear from readers. Connect with Lisa at lisacarterauthor.com.

Books by Lisa Carter

Love Inspired

Coast Guard Courtship
Coast Guard Sweetheart
Falling for the Single Dad
The Deputy's Perfect Match
The Bachelor's Unexpected Family
The Christmas Baby
Hometown Reunion
His Secret Daughter

Visit the Author Profile page at Harlequin.com.

His Secret
Daughter

Lisa Carter

Recycling programs
for this product may
not exist in your area.

LOVE INSPIRED BOOKS

ISBN-13: 978-1-335-53907-6

His Secret Daughter

Copyright © 2019 by Lisa Carter

A word fitly spoken is like apples of gold
in pictures of silver.
—*Proverbs* 25:11

Much thanks to Red and Joan Price and Melissa, Megan and Chris Pendergraft at Mountain Fresh Orchards in Hendersonville, North Carolina. Thanks for helping me understand the intricacies of growing apples and for the tour of your beautiful orchard. Any errors are my own.

Chapter One

Jake McAbee didn't know much, but he did know when he was in the middle of nowhere.

A place he'd been before. Many times, in fact. Like the derelict trailer park where he'd grown up. Or the jagged peaks of an Afghan mountain range. And today on a deserted road somewhere in the Blue Ridge Mountains of North Carolina.

He slowed the truck, going as far as the pavement allowed on the dead-end road. Performing a U-turn, he cranked the wheel hard. If only getting free of his dead-end life was as easy as turning his truck around.

Sighing, he palmed the wheel and headed out the way he'd come. He should've gone left at the fork. A mistake soon rectified. If only everything else wrong in his life was as easily fixed.

Jake set his jaw. No more of that. The past needed to stay in the past. He was on his way to meet his baby girl for the first time. A child he'd learned about just a few months ago.

Her mother had kept Maisie's existence from him, a fact that opened a hollow place in his heart. He'd missed the first two and a half years of her life.

But when Tiffany died—too young—of breast cancer, her best friend, Callie Jackson, had notified him that he had a daughter. He had been on a mission in a remote region of Afghanistan, so it had taken the army a while to get ahold of him.

Gripping the wheel, he veered at the fork. He owed Callie big-time. Not only had she cared for his ex-wife during her illness, she'd also practically raised his daughter by herself in the last few months since Tiff's death.

He let out a breath, uncurling one hand. Flexing his fingers, he released his death grip on the steering wheel. Trying to relax. Trying to breathe.

Even now, he could hardly believe he had a daughter. The thought filled him with both elation and fear. Fear that he'd fail Maisie as he'd failed her mother. But also joy for his precious daughter and the new beginning he was determined to make for them.

A brand-new, wonderful life with his child.

The towering peaks of the tree-studded Blue Ridge flashed by on either side of his truck. Descending into the valley, he emerged into slightly gentler terrain. The rolled hay bales of late summer dotted grassy meadows. Horses grazed in the pastures, and there was row after row of orchards. Callie had said the area was known for its apples.

Per her directions, he skirted the town and its welcome marker proclaiming Truelove, North Carolina—Where True Love Awaits. But after his failed marriage—once burned, twice shy—the only true love he was interested in was the love of the daughter he had yet to meet.

A couple of miles later he spotted the turnoff. Apple Valley Farm, a weathered sign read. He pulled off the main highway through the crossbars. Bypassing a rustic country store, he continued on the long gravel-covered road. The apple trees lining the driveway were heavy with ripening fruit. Queen Anne's lace and purple wildflowers studded a nearby meadow.

Overlooking the orchard, the tin roof of the two-story white farmhouse set high on a knoll gleamed in the afternoon sun and caused his breath to hitch. River stones lined the solid foundation and chimney. And at the heart of this home, a red-painted door bade a welcome to all.

He braked on the incline, and dust swirled. An unfamiliar sensation burned in his chest. He'd never had a real home, certainly not one he was proud of. But if he'd ever imagined—dreamed—

what home would look like, it might have resembled the Jackson farm.

Jake's stomach twisted. More than ever, he was glad Maisie had spent the first two years of her life here. One thing Tiffany had done right—coming to the orchard during her illness and then after her death leaving their daughter with the very capable Callie Jackson.

Today he'd meet his daughter for the first time. But suppose Maisie didn't like him? Suppose—

Stop stalling, McAbee.

He took a deep breath, easing his foot off the brake. He parked beside a blue Chevy sedan, a pink car seat strapped into the back seat. Thrusting open the truck door, he stepped out, his work boots crunching on the pebbled stone.

A slim woman in a lavender shirt came out of the house onto the broad-planked porch. A year or two younger than his own twenty-eight years, she was tallish even in flats, perhaps five foot seven or so to his six-foot height. Masses of long auburn hair waved across her shoulders and framed her heart-shaped face.

He recognized her from the photo in which she'd held his daughter. For the first time, he wondered who'd taken the picture. She'd never mentioned a husband. And before he could stop himself, his eyes darted to her left hand, clenched against her crisp jeans. Was she as nervous as he was?

Jake shut the dinging truck door with a soft click. He didn't move. Neither did Callie. But he waited for her to invite him over, as she'd invited him to come to Truelove and meet his daughter. Upon learning of his daughter's existence and finishing his enlistment, he'd chosen not to re-up and had flown stateside.

"Hi, Jake." At the thready note in her voice, Callie cleared her throat. "Welcome to Apple Valley Farm."

Jake halted at the base of the steps. "Hi, Callie. And thank you." His turn to swallow. "For everything."

She knotted her hands together. Her lovely brown eyes were red rimmed. She'd been crying.

His heart banged against his rib cage. She'd been crying because of him. Because he'd come to claim his daughter, to take Maisie away forever.

"I'm sorry," she whispered, swiping a finger under her eye. "I've been trying not to let Maisie see me like this. It's just so…" She bit her lip.

"None of this is your fault, Callie."

She raised her tear-filled gaze to his, and his heart thudded. What was wrong with him? It wasn't like Jake to get emotional.

He'd learned the hard way—and early—never to get too attached. He must be tired. It had been a long drive from Fort Bragg to the mountains.

She unknotted her hands, smoothing her shirt. "It's not your fault, either, Jake."

He wasn't sure that was entirely true. He'd spent years going over every detail of his short-lived union with Tiffany, but he'd never figured out what caused her to walk away from their marriage.

Jake grimaced. "Tiffany should've never put you in this position. Maisie should've never been your responsibility."

"Maisie has never been a burden." Callie lifted her chin. "She's the joy of my life."

The front door creaked. An older man in his late fifties poked his head around the frame. "Maisie's wondering where you are, honey." He had the classic kind of blond attractiveness that aged well.

Callie took a shuddery breath. "Jake, this is my father, Nash." She gestured. "Dad, meet Jake McAbee, Maisie's father."

Nash's dark eyes took on a steely glint. "Takes more than biology to be a dad."

Callie gasped. "Daddy."

It was something Jake had learned firsthand from his own deadbeat dad.

"Your father's right." He met Nash Jackson's gaze head-on. "I didn't know about Maisie before. But now…" He inhaled. "Now I intend to be not just her father, but her dad, too."

Callie motioned. "Come inside, Jake."

He followed her across the veranda. Boxes were stacked on the porch. A child-size suitcase. And what appeared to be a deconstructed crib.

In the distance, he spied the smoky haze of the Blue Ridge vista. The wraparound porch allowed for incredible three-sixty views from every vantage point. Sunsets must be spectacular.

She shouldered past her dad in the doorway. For a second he wondered if Nash would let him through, but her father stepped aside.

"I'll be out here." Nash shoved off. "Loading Maisie's things. Including the car seat." He wasn't talking to Callie. He was warning Jake.

Behind the anger was also fear and hurt. Nash Jackson loved Maisie. It was Nash who'd given Jake's child a safe, stable home.

For that, Jake was grateful. And he was sorry for the pain his coming would bring the Jacksons, who'd done nothing but love his child.

Stepping across the threshold, Jake found himself in a small foyer. Rooms bookended either side of the hall. Rigid with tension, Callie waited for him at the bottom of the staircase.

"Cawee!" a little girl called from the back of the house.

His heart went into overdrive. "Is that—" A lump formed in his throat.

Callie tilted her head. "I told her she was going to meet her daddy today."

He had a hard time catching his breath.

Callie motioned him down the hallway. "She's playing in the family room."

The family room ran the length of the house. Windows lined the wall, spilling sunshine into the adjoining kitchen. And judging from the toys littering the pinewood floors, the room also served as a child's playroom. But despite a quick scan, he failed to spot his daughter.

A teasing look on her pretty features, Callie propped her hands on her hips. "Where, oh, where is Maisie Nicole McAbee?" she called in a singsong voice. "Where, oh, where can she be?"

"Me here, Cawee."

A childish giggle erupted from behind the leather recliner, and a small child—all blond, bouncing curls—burst forth, her arms capturing Callie around the knees. His heart leaped in his chest.

Callie kissed the top of the child's—his child's—head. "Someone's here to see you, baby girl. Don't be shy. Your daddy's come a long way to meet you."

Slowly, the little girl raised her head. The photograph Callie sent hadn't begun to capture the true essence of his daughter. With her finger stuck in the corner of her rosebud mouth, she contemplated her father with eyes so blue he feared he might drown in their azure depths.

And, perhaps for the first time in his life, Jake McAbee truly fell hopelessly—helplessly—in love.

Callie watched the play of emotion across the ruggedly handsome soldier's face. Was Jake McAbee a man who could be trusted with the well-being of the child she loved more than life itself?

Maisie leaned against Callie while taking measure of her soldier father. Pain knifed through Callie's heart. How could she bear to never see Maisie again? To not watch her grow up? To not be a part of her life?

But the vulnerability and unconditional love in Jake McAbee's face surprised Callie. In the photograph he'd sent of himself, he'd worn sand-colored combat fatigues, and an aloofness, too.

A self-protective mechanism? A facade? If so, what had driven him to hide his real feelings?

War? Or his failed relationship with his wife, Callie's childhood friend, Tiff? Maybe both. Though Tiff had hinted that Jake's remoteness predated her ever meeting the young soldier stationed in Fayetteville.

No longer in uniform, he trembled slightly, swaying on the balls of his feet. Shirtsleeves rolled to his elbows revealed thickly corded forearms. His Adam's apple bobbed above the open collar of his button-down, untucked shirt.

A shirt as blue as his eyes. As blue as Maisie's. She glanced from the child to the man. The two of them were locked in a silent, long-overdue perusal of each other.

There could be no doubt Maisie belonged to Jake McAbee. The shape of her face. Underneath the bearded scruff on Jake's jawline, a similar dimple in their chins. The nose.

Or was she merely seeing what she wanted to see?

She pushed aside her doubts about what Tiff had and hadn't said. When Tiff had arrived at Apple Valley Farm she was already sick and pregnant. Callie had been by her side when Maisie was born. But in typical Tiff fashion, it had fallen to Callie to sort out the mess she'd left unfinished at her death a few months ago.

Jake's name was on the birth certificate, but Tiff hadn't always told the truth. Callie's loyalty to her friend had warred with what was right. But she'd made it a lifetime habit to always do what was right. So after much prayer, she'd finally contacted Maisie's father.

Still, she hadn't figured on how doing the right thing would hurt so much. She cupped the crown of Maisie's silken head in her palm. And now… She wasn't sure how she was going to give Maisie up.

Jake went down on one knee. His eyes never left his daughter's face, but he was careful not to touch Maisie.

He propped his arm on his thigh. "Hi, Maisie," he rasped. "You are the most beautiful little girl I've ever seen."

Callie's heart warmed to the ex-soldier. Maisie was everything and more a parent could ever ask for. Smart and kind, a furious ball of energy.

Maisie let go of Callie's legs. She immediately felt the loss of the child's warmth, a harbinger of the future. She wrung her hands.

The little girl pointed her index finger to the photo of Jake on the bookcase. "My daddy?"

He choked off a half sob. "Yes, baby. I am your daddy, and I am so happy to finally meet you."

Callie's eyes misted. He loved Maisie. This was what she'd been hoping for, praying for, ever since she contacted the army. But her arms ached with a coming emptiness. Her heart was breaking.

This is the right thing, isn't it, God? Her precious child would be all right. *Won't she, God? A girl needs her dad. Doesn't she?*

Maisie inched toward her beloved miniature barn. Reaching inside, she withdrew a tiny plastic farmer. Golden curls brushed Maisie's shoulders as she held it out to Jake. "Pway with me?"

He stared at her a second, not realizing he'd

been given an invitation. But when he did, he nearly fell over himself crawling to the barnyard.

Sinking onto the leather ottoman, Callie watched as they played together. Actually, Maisie played and Jake, her adoring servant, moved things where Maisie told him to put them. Maisie had already captured his heart.

Maisie ran the green tractor over the circular rag rug. "Me big-gull bed." She arched her tiny eyebrow at her father. "No mow cwib."

Jake cocked his head. "What, Maisie?"

Callie smiled. "She's been after us to take her out of the crib and get her a big-girl bed."

He leaned on his elbows. "But you don't think it's a good idea?"

"We've been so busy getting the orchard ready for harvest, I haven't had time to look into it. Maybe soon, though."

He nodded and his focus returned to his daughter.

Despite his short military haircut, she could imagine how his dirty-blond hair could've easily been the same buttery blond as his daughter's when he was her age. Awe shone out of his eyes as he gazed at Maisie. And, when he glanced over to Callie, gratitude, also.

"Maybe you should go over her schedule with me, Callie."

She blinked. Her heart pounded. Not yet. She

wasn't ready. Although would she ever be ready to relinquish Maisie?

Was Jake the father Maisie needed? Callie had had him investigated before contacting the military after Tiff died.

From humble beginnings in Texas, Jake McAbee had joined the army right out of high school, where he'd excelled in almost every sport. An excellence he brought to the army, serving his country with distinction.

He was a three-tour combat veteran, well spoken of by his commanding officers and the men with whom he served. By all accounts, he was a good man who hadn't deserved what Tiff had done to him.

Callie closed her eyes. There she went again. But Tiff had made poor choice after poor choice as long as Callie had known her.

Perhaps one of Tiff's biggest mistakes had been filing divorce on her young husband of two months while Jake was deployed.

"Uh, Callie?"

She opened her eyes.

"I booked a motel room tonight in Asheville. I didn't want to drive over the mountains in the dark on unfamiliar roads."

Ready or not, Jake was Maisie's father. She'd hoped to convince him to stay the night at the orchard to give Maisie more time to adjust. But

Asheville wasn't far. She was on shaky ground here. If she pushed too hard, too soon...

"I've packed her clothes." Callie rose. "And most of her toys."

His lips curved, and something like the sweep of butterfly wings fluttered in her belly.

Jake gestured at the living room. "She's got more than this?"

Callie gave him a small smile. "You, Sergeant, have a lot to learn about girls."

The light dimmed in his eyes, and his mouth flattened. "I think Tiffany walking out on me underscores how little I actually know about women."

"Jake, I didn't mean—"

He rose abruptly. "But I'm a quick learner." His broad shoulders tapered to the narrow waist above his jeans.

The clean, spicy scent of his male presence robbed Callie of coherent thought. This was ridiculous. A person would think she'd never been around a man before.

Although none so...so male as Jake McAbee.

"Callie?"

She jerked.

"Maisie's schedule?"

She seized on the first thing that came to her mind—food. "Maisie usually has a snack around this time. Goldfish."

Maisie's head popped up over the wooden barn. "Fish?"

Callie nodded. "And apple juice."

Maisie smiled, wrenching Callie's heart. "'Appy juice."

"Happy juice, huh?" He gave Callie a grudging smile. "What else at Apple Valley Farm?"

Strolling into the adjacent kitchen, she poured the juice into a sippy cup. "Apple juice makes everyone happy."

Maisie stood beside the farmhouse table, waiting to be hoisted into her booster seat, strapped to one of the chairs. The booster was yet another item Callie had forgotten to pack. Maisie's possessions were scattered throughout the house, blending in with the other furnishings. Belonging.

Jake raised his hands to lift Maisie into the booster seat, but stopped short of touching her. His brow scrunched. "Will she let me put her in the seat?"

Callie took a deep breath. Now for the test. "Let's try." She injected an over-the-top note of cheer into her voice. "Can Daddy put you in your big-girl seat, Maisie?"

There was a long second where Callie held her breath. Probably Jake, too.

"'Kay."

The relief on his face was poignant. Callie's

head insisted this was the best possible outcome. But her heart…?

Maisie held her arms up to her father. And as if afraid he'd break her, he gingerly lifted his daughter.

For a fraction of a heartbeat, he held her against himself, breathing in the little-girl fragrance of his daughter. The fresh-out-of-the-bath, baby-shampoo smell. A scent that, after today, Callie would never know again. Sudden tears blinded her, and she spilled some of the apple juice on the counter. After that split-second pause, just as gently, Jake deposited Maisie into the booster seat. Flustered, Callie carried the green sippy cup to Maisie.

"Daddy wikes gween." Maisie quirked her eyebrow. "Wight, Cawee?"

Jake's eyes cut to her.

She flushed. "That's right, Maisie. Your daddy's favorite color is green."

"I'm surprised Tiffany remembered. Did she ever talk to you about me? Did she ever explain why—" His voice went hollow.

"Only bits and pieces." She moistened her bottom lip. If she wasn't careful, she'd become like Tiff—a liar. "I'm sorry, Jake."

"You have absolutely nothing to be sorry about, Callie." There was pain in his voice. In his eyes, too.

But she *was* sorry. At the moment, sorry that

she'd done the right thing in contacting Jake McAbee. There had to be something—anything—she could do or say to make him change his mind about taking Maisie away.

She took hold of his arm. At the touch of his skin against hers, something sparked. A tingling sensation ran from her hand up to her elbow. She drew back.

"Please, Jake," she whispered. "Please don't take Maisie from the only home she's ever known."

His blue eyes flickered. "She and I will make a new home together."

Callie's gut tightened. "I'm begging you to think of what's best for Maisie, Jake."

His face went hard. "I *am* thinking of what's best for Maisie."

At the sound of her name, Maisie looked up, the cup spout between her lips.

"Being with her father is what's best for Maisie," he growled.

Callie grabbed on to the spindles of the chair. "But where are you taking her, Jake?"

His eyes narrowed. "A friend in Houston is hiring workers for an oil rig."

"Texas?" She'd been thinking, hoping, maybe he'd settle nearby. "What do you plan to do with her while you're out on an oil rig for days at a time?"

A muscle ticked in his cheek. "I'll make sure

she's safe and cared for." The look he gave Callie wasn't friendly. "But I won't let anyone ever keep me from my daughter again. She's mine."

Despite common sense telling Callie she needed to let this go, she couldn't. Not for Maisie's sake. Not for her own.

"Maisie isn't a thing to be possessed, Jake. She doesn't know you. If you leave now she's going to be scared. You could damage your relationship with her for good."

He went completely still. This man was a soldier. He could be dangerous, especially to anyone he perceived as a threat. But she couldn't stop now, not when Maisie's well-being hung in the balance.

"We could visit you in Houston over Christmas. Let Maisie learn to trust you—love you—in her own way and time. Please, I'm begging you to do the right thing."

Sucking in a breath, he crossed his arms over his well-muscled chest. "The right thing?"

At the anger lacing their raised voices, Maisie let out a whimper.

His jaw jutted. "How dare you lecture me on the right thing. How long have you known I was Maisie's father?"

She dropped her eyes, not able to meet his gaze. "Since Tiff filled out the birth certificate."

He loomed over Maisie, getting in Callie's

space. "And how hard did you try to convince Tiffany to do the right thing by me?" He was so close his breath fanned her face.

She stood her ground, not giving an inch. Maisie's future was at stake. And everyone's happiness. Everyone, except Jake? She hardened her heart. She couldn't let him take Maisie.

"Tiff wouldn't listen."

He gave a short bark of a laugh. More bitter disillusionment than mirth. "Why doesn't that surprise me?"

Maisie's big blue eyes ping-ponged between them. "Cawee?" Her bottom lip trembled.

"You're already scaring her." She placed her hand on Maisie's shoulder and curled her lip. "What kind of father does that, Jake McAbee?"

Something flashed across his face, something raw, evoking a reluctant compassion in her tender heart. But she mustn't weaken. "I won't let you take her." She gritted her teeth.

"You can't stop me," he growled. "I'm within my parental rights, and you know it." In a swift, unexpected move, he lifted Maisie out of the booster seat.

Maisie and Callie cried out at the same time.

"I'll figure everything out as I go." Clasping the squirming child close, he strode toward the hall. "We're leaving."

"No, Jake. Stop." Callie ran after him. "Don't leave this way. She won't understand."

Maisie's little arms grasped the air over his shoulder, stretching toward Callie. "Cawee! Cawee!"

He flung open the door. Leaning against the porch railing, her father startled at the commotion.

Callie's chest heaved. "Dad, don't let him take her."

Her father's features sagged. "She's his child, Callie. Not ours."

Jake rushed down the steps. Like a wild thing, Maisie thrashed in his arms.

Callie plunged after them. But catching her around the waist, her father held Callie on the porch. "Don't make this worse, honey."

She didn't see how this could be much worse. She strained against her father's grasp. "Maisie!"

How had it come to this? How had this escalated so far out of control? *God, where are You?*

Chapter Two

Somehow Jake managed to wrangle his daughter into the car seat Nash had secured in the truck cab.

"Cawee!" she shrieked. "Cawee!"

He flinched but made sure the buckles clicked in place. Rounding the hood, he slid behind the wheel and cranked the engine. Nausea roiled in his stomach.

This wasn't the way he'd wanted things to go, but Callie's words had touched a nerve. He would show them all. He would be the best dad Maisie never had. He wouldn't desert her or belittle her like his father—

Jake threw the truck into gear, glancing at the house in the rearview mirror. Seeing Nash Jackson's arm draped around her, Callie weeping, almost broke Jake. He'd never wanted to hurt her. This was killing her. *He* was killing her.

Tears streaming across her cheeks, she sank

onto the porch step. And the last thing he glimpsed before the truck sped over the rise was Callie burying her face in her hands.

Gritting his teeth, he barreled past the shuttered country store and set his face forward toward the road beyond the crossbars of the farm. In the seat behind him, Maisie's cries had subsided into heart-wrenching, hopeless sobs.

"No, D-Daddy," she hiccupped. "Bad, bad Daddy."

Jake slammed on the brakes, spinning gravel. Bad daddy. Like his father. Though he'd promised himself he'd never do anything to hurt his child.

He pressed his forehead against the wheel. What was he doing? What had he done to his daughter except terrify her? Callie was right.

No matter how much he wanted to be her dad, he couldn't tear Maisie away from the only home she'd ever known. From everything that made her feel safe. From everyone who loved her. He didn't have it in him to put his rights over Maisie's happiness. Not if he truly loved Maisie…

Jake loved her more than himself, loved her the way no one in his life had ever loved him. A soul-deep kind of love, impossible to ever find. But that had never stopped him from hungering for it anyway.

He couldn't do this to Maisie. Not this way. Not now.

For the second time that day, he turned the truck around. He parked once more beside the blue Chevy sedan. The Jacksons hadn't moved from the porch. They stared at him, mute and motionless. Shoulders hunched, he stepped out and rounded the hood. Opening the truck door, he leaned in, but Maisie shrank from him.

And his heart broke.

He steeled himself to do the hard thing, the right thing, for Maisie. She was the only one who mattered in this situation. As for him? Like always, he'd do his mourning in private.

Jake made short work of the buckles. Maisie stiffened when he lifted her out of the seat. Nevertheless, with his daughter cradled in his arms, like an old man, he stumbled toward the Jacksons. When he reached the steps, Callie rose, and he gave his daughter to her.

His child—no, Callie's child—burrowed into her. With small, sniffling noises, Maisie pressed her face into the hollow of Callie's shoulder.

"Oh, Maisie, sweetheart. Callie's here. Don't cry."

"I'm sorry. I shouldn't have taken her like that." His voice guttural, he kept his gaze pinned on the grass. "I won't ever bother you again. Maisie belongs here with you, not with me. I'll send money. I—I won't be a deadbeat dad." Clamping his lips together, he started to turn away.

"Wait. Jake."

Midmotion, he froze.

"Don't go." Callie stretched out her hand to him. "Please stay."

"Callie Girl, what are you doing?" Nash grunted.

"It—it's not right, him leaving. I can't let it end this way."

Nash's gaze flickered between Jake and his daughter.

Jake steeled himself against the whisper of hope unfurling inside his chest. "I don't understand. I figured you couldn't wait to be rid of me for good. What are you saying?"

"I'm asking you to stay on the farm." She lifted her chin. "A temporary arrangement so that you and Maisie can become better acquainted. Where she feels comfortable and safe."

"Why would you want me to stay?" Jake frowned. "After what I did."

Maisie shrank away from him as Callie closed the distance between them on the grass. "Because maybe if Tiff had had a dad who…" She moistened her lips. "I won't allow history to repeat itself. A girl needs her father, Jake."

She shifted Maisie onto the crook of her other arm as the child almost strangled Callie in her effort to stay as far from Jake as possible.

Anguish clawed at his insides, but he was going to have to learn to live with the gnawing pain of having lost his daughter. As he'd learned to live with the pain of Tiffany's rejection.

"What would be the point, Callie? Maisie will never trust me again."

She touched his arm, surprising him. And myriad emotions exploded in his chest, feelings he didn't care to examine too closely. After the way he'd failed Tiffany and now Maisie, too, these were emotions he had no business feeling.

"Trust can be rebuilt, Jake. You and Maisie need time."

He shook his head. "Time is something I don't have. Exactly what are you suggesting? I have to find work."

"Apple harvest has just begun…" Her gaze darted to her father. "You need help in the orchard. Right, Dad?"

Nash's face had become unreadable, but finally he nodded. "I haven't fully regained my stamina after being hospitalized for pneumonia last winter."

The smile she threw her father caused Jake's gut to clench. It was a smile Jake in no way deserved or could ever hope to receive from his own daughter.

Nash folded his arms across his chest. "Gala and Honeycrisp apples come off first. We open the farm to the public this weekend for Labor Day."

"I don't have many job skills suited for civilian life." Jake ground his teeth. "But I won't take charity."

"No charity here." Nash jutted his jaw. "It's hard, honest work. We're slammed with visitors during harvest season. The orchard is more than Callie and I can handle alone."

She took another step in Jake's direction. "We could use your help. Julio, Dad's right-hand man for over a decade, recently moved east to be near his grandchildren."

Despite his ingrained defenses, hope took slow root in his heart. "Let me make sure I understand this deal you're offering me. I work the harvest and in exchange, I get to spend more time with Maisie?"

She bit her lip. "Please, Jake. For Maisie's sake. And yours."

He widened his stance. "And, after that, you'd want me to leave."

Callie narrowed her eyes at him. "Like I said, a temporary arrangement."

Staying would mean inevitable heartache once the harvest was over, yet how could he refuse a second chance with his daughter? He longed for nothing more than to know his child.

"How much time are we talking about here?" He raked his hand over his head. "I can't put my buddy off forever."

"By Thanksgiving, apple season is over, and

Maisie will have gotten used to you." Callie threw him a dazzling smile, momentarily blinding Jake. "You'll see. Children forgive and forget far easier than grown-ups."

Tucked into the curve of Callie's neck, Maisie regarded him with accusatory eyes.

Oh, how he hoped Callie was right. He prayed she was right. Pray—something he should've done before grabbing his child.

His stomach knotted. "If you're sure…"

"I'm sure. Do we have a deal?"

A deal on Callie's terms and at Maisie's pace. Yet, what other choice did his heart really have? He'd take what he could get of Maisie.

"We have a deal." He swallowed. "I'll be gone by Thanksgiving."

"Right. Gone by Thanksgiving." She started up the steps. "Give me a few minutes to get your room ready."

"You want me to stay here?" His head snapped back. "In your house?"

"Time isn't on our side. The clock's ticking on apple season and on creating a real relationship with your daughter." After wrenching open the door, the hinges squeaking, she and Maisie disappeared inside the house.

Only then did Nash Jackson move, his boots a heavy tread on the boards. When they were shoulder to shoulder, Callie's father paused, locking gazes with Jake. What Jake read there told him to proceed with caution.

His eyes dark like obsidian, Nash had gone still. A tightly leashed control Jake recognized and respected.

"If you hurt *my* child, Jake McAbee—" the threat made more menacing by Nash's quiet, deceptively conversational tone "—I'll make sure it's the last thing you ever do on this mountain."

Callie went all out for supper.

The summer garden was about played out at this point. She'd been canning, freezing and pickling since July. She was secretly gratified to see Jake's eyes widen as she placed one dish after the other on the table. Cream corn, butter beans, sweet pickles, mashed potatoes, biscuits and fried chicken.

She sank into the chair opposite Jake, within arm's reach of Maisie in the booster seat. At the head of the table, her father said grace.

Puckering her lips, Maisie scooped corn onto her spoon and more or less managed to find her mouth. A smile flitted across Jake's handsome lips.

Handsome— What was wrong with her?

Callie lowered her eyes to her plate. He was Maisie's father. It didn't matter whether he had handsome lips or not.

With an upsweep of her lashes, she stole another look at him. But he did. He definitely had handsome lips.

Jake shoveled mashed potatoes onto his plate. "You eat like this every day, Mr. Jackson?"

Her father reached for another chicken leg. "Like her mother, Callie has a way around the kitchen."

"She sure does. I haven't eaten this good since…ever."

Callie fretted the paper napkin in her lap. "Your mother didn't like to cook?"

Shrugging, he helped himself to the bowl of butter beans. "Don't remember much before she was gone."

Callie took the bowl from him and set it down on the table. "I was in college when my mom died. How old were you when your mother died?"

"Didn't say she died." His shoulders tensed, but he didn't look up. "When I was nine, she just left."

Like Tiff.

Callie's breath hitched. His tone bothered her the most. It was as matter-of-fact as if talking about the weather.

He split open a steaming-hot biscuit. Brows drawn, her dad passed Jake the butter dish. Jake slathered both sides of the biscuit with butter.

"So how did your mother die, Callie?" With a sudden clang, he laid the knife across his plate.

"I shouldn't have asked that, Mr. Jackson. None of my business."

Her dad laid down his fork. "Cancer. And we don't mind talking about her. Keeps her memory alive."

Callie handed Jake a small mason jar of strawberry jam. "I came home to take care of my mom—" she smiled at her father "—and decided everything I wanted was right here."

Jake spooned jam onto his biscuit. "First your mom. Then Tiffany. Always taking care of other people." He caught her eye. "The hits just kept coming, didn't they, Callie?"

Their gazes locked across the table.

She had a feeling Jake knew more than she about taking hits.

Her dad cleared his throat. Jolted, she became aware that Maisie was studying Jake with those blue, blue eyes of hers.

Sippy cup hanging loosely in one hand, Maisie watched as the men discussed the upcoming harvest and what needed to be done in the orchard.

But without fail, Jake's attention returned to his daughter, like he couldn't get enough of her. Starving—Callie realized—in more ways than one. His longing for his child was so evident, something unfamiliar—and not altogether welcome—stirred inside Callie.

It wouldn't do to get too sympathetic toward Jake McAbee. Legally, he had the right to take the custody issue to court. A court battle was something the Jacksons could neither afford nor win. He still possessed the power to take Maisie away from them. She was running a risk in letting him stay.

So why then, when he'd been willing to walk away, had she offered him a job? She swallowed past the sudden lump in her throat. She wasn't sure why she'd done that.

Except for an overwhelming feeling that she couldn't let him leave. Was it a sense of guilt about waiting so long to do the right thing by him and Maisie? For continuing to keep Tiff's secret? Or something else?

Callie brushed a stray blond curl out of Maisie's face.

"I missed her baby stage." Sadness clouded Jake's features. "I guess I've missed a lot of other things, too."

Callie and her father exchanged glances. A strained silence hung over the table while they digested that irreversible truth.

Her dad withdrew a pen from his shirt pocket, sketching on his napkin the boundary lines of the farm. "Here's the orchard layout."

Jake cocked his head, examining the rough drawing. "How many acres do you farm, sir?"

She could tell, despite himself, her father was impressed by the *sir*.

"Ten. We grow Jonathan apples, Red Delicious

and Golden in the rows to the right of the house. In September, we'll harvest those."

When she rose to clear the table, so did Jake. "Let me help, Callie."

His mother might've abandoned Jake McAbee when he was young, but someone had instilled in him gentlemanly manners.

She waved him away. "You and Dad finish talking."

With reluctance, Jake sat down again and pointed to a square on the napkin. "What's the building by the road?"

"The Apple House." Her father patted his stomach. "My favorite place on the farm."

She scraped the plates. "The orchard is your favorite place on the farm."

Her father laughed. "True."

Jake leaned on the armrest of the chair. "What's an apple house?"

She stacked the plates. "A country store and bakery."

"That's why it's my second-favorite place on the farm." Her dad smiled at her. "Once we open the orchard to the public, Callie has a seasonal crew of town ladies who run the storefront and keep it stocked with apple doughnuts, pies and fritters for sale."

She carried the dishes to the sink, then returned with a wet cloth to wipe Maisie's hands. Twisting her head from side to side like every night, Maisie fought Callie's efforts to wipe her mouth.

But Callie wasn't a quitter and she persevered. Just as she did every night. "Late October also brings the Apple Festival for the farmers in the valley."

"Any experience driving a tractor or using farm equipment, Jake?" Her father pursed his lips. "Every weekend from September till we close mid-November, we offer hayrides when people come to buy our apples. For school groups during the week, too."

Maisie perked up in her booster seat. "Twactor?"

Callie looked at Jake. "Maisie likes the tractor. A lot."

Jake gathered the silverware into a bundle for Callie. "Overseas I did some convoy driving."

Her father quirked his brow. "Then I suspect if you can drive around IEDs and insurgents, you can handle a hayride." He sniffed the air. "Was that cobbler I smelled baking earlier, Callie Girl?"

She grinned. "Blackberry."

Maisie raised her arms. "Pop-Pop?"

Callie's dad reddened. "I realize I'm not her grandfather, but she started calling me that one day. I should've set her straight, but—"

"You're the only grandparent she'll ever know."

Jake sighed. "I'm glad she's had a strong man like you in her life."

With a thoughtful expression in his eyes, Callie's father scraped back his chair. "And now she'll have two strong men in her life."

"Thank you, sir." Jake squared his shoulders. "That means a lot to me."

Her dad lifted Maisie into his arms. "We'll be back 'fore long to eat that cobbler, Callie Girl." He tickled Maisie's belly. "Right, Daisy Maisie?"

Maisie crumpled into giggles.

Callie couldn't help smiling. "Dad likes to work off supper by taking a sunset stroll with Maisie through the orchard."

Her father winked at Jake. "Got to start those farm girls young." With Maisie hanging on to his neck, they headed outside, the screen door slamming behind them.

Suddenly alone with Jake, she went around to the other side of the table to give herself breathing room. His strong, masculine presence made her feel like a stammering schoolgirl.

He was a man with questions about Maisie's mother she couldn't answer. Because the answers were emotional land mines with enough fallout to devastate them all. She wiped down the booster seat.

What invitation to disaster had she already

set into motion by asking Jake to stick around? Callie gripped Maisie's chair. This wouldn't— couldn't—end well.

Secrets never did.

Chapter Three

Clearing the dining table, Jake reached for the empty glass at the same time as Callie. She blushed furiously. He let go immediately and stepped out of her way. What about him made her so uncomfortable? Or, like Maisie, did she hate him, too?

Jake didn't blame her for not trusting him after what happened earlier with Maisie. So why had she asked him to stay, even temporarily? Sometimes when she looked at him, genuine warmth shone out of her lovely brown eyes; other times, she wore an expression he didn't know how to interpret.

He followed her into the kitchen. "Let me dry while you wash."

Standing at the sink, she kept her back to him. "No."

He scrunched his brow. "Bossy, aren't you?"

She angled her head and made a face. "Hence my single status, I suppose."

He leaned against the counter. "Guys around here must be blind, then." He shifted. What had possessed him to say such a thing to her?

She flushed twelve shades of red, the way only a redhead could, and she set to scouring the pot with enough force to take the finish off. "You're a flirt."

He stiffened. "Did Tiffany say that about me? Because I'm not. After we were married, brief as it was, I never... Is that why she left? Is that what she told you?"

Callie stopped scrubbing and looked at him. "The only thing I know for sure, Jake McAbee, is that Maisie needs a father."

She hadn't answered his question about Tiffany. He let it go for now.

"The only thing I know for sure, Callie Jackson, is that we both love Maisie."

Her eyes became luminous. "Yes." She focused on the pan in the sink. "Yes, we do."

Finding a cloth, he dried the dishes in the drainer. They worked in silence, each lost in their own thoughts. After everything had been put away, she straightened, seeming to come to a sudden decision.

She started toward the living room. "I have something to show you."

His heart pounded.

"Please take a seat." She motioned to the

couch. "This will take a while." She removed two leather-bound albums from the bookcase.

An expensive camera with a denim strap sat on the top shelf, placed out of Maisie's reach, but easily accessible for adults, he guessed.

She sank onto the sofa, keeping a respectable distance. He caught a whiff of her perfume, a pleasing fruity fragrance, reminding him of apples. Callie placed the albums on the coffee table in front of him.

Leaning forward, he rested his elbows on his knees. "What are these?"

"Maisie's life in pictures, thus far." Callie swallowed. "I can't give you back the time you lost with her, but I can give you a glimpse into those years."

He stared at her. "I don't know what I did that made Tiffany leave. I wish I did."

The unvoiced question lay between them, again giving Callie the option to answer. Or not.

She handed him the album on top of the pile. "I like taking photos, so I documented everything I could."

Apparently, choosing not.

He wasn't prepared for the rush of disappointment that flooded him. Would he be around long enough to earn her trust? And why did it matter so much?

* * *

It wasn't right to let him believe he was to blame for what happened to his marriage. Guilt knotted her stomach, but her deathbed promise to Tiff bound Callie to silence. And a new anger burned against her dead friend for the impossible position in which Tiff had placed her.

Maybe someday she'd tell him what happened with Tiff, but for now, she couldn't. She didn't know Jake McAbee well enough for those kinds of revelations. She didn't know how he'd handle the truth. She also didn't know him well enough yet to hurt him that much.

But photos she could do. She opened to the first page in the album.

The photograph of newborn Maisie completely captured Jake, and he let the subject drop. For how long, though?

"You take great pictures, Callie." He smiled, the lines at the corners of his eyes fanning out in warmth. "You could turn professional."

"Only a hobby." Shaking her head, she rose. "Take your time. I usually join Dad and Maisie on their walk in the orchard."

Professional photography was a daydream she'd put behind her long ago. First her mother's illness, then Tiff's. Most recently, her dad's.

Her father couldn't manage the orchard without her, and Maisie needed her.

Remembering she hadn't put any towels in Jake's bathroom, she detoured upstairs. One of the best things about summer were the long hours of daylight stretching into the evening. There was plenty of time to catch the sunset with her dad and Maisie.

A few minutes later when she returned to the front hall, she heard a strangled sound from the living room. Jake? Had something happened while she was upstairs?

Light-footed with urgency, she got as far as the kitchen before a sight she'd never forget froze Callie in her tracks.

The photo album lay open to happy pictures of his daughter's first Christmas, first birthday, first toothy grin. Jake's face was buried in his hands, and his shoulders shook with muffled, bone-jarring sobs. His body was racked with grief and pain.

Something tore inside her chest.

To spare Jake his pride, she tiptoed out, retreating to the hallway. After easing open the front door, she slipped outside.

Her legs unable to support her, she leaned against the porch column, trying to regain her breath. Trying to still her racing heart. Trying not to lose her supper.

She had never hated anyone in her life, but right now she hated more than anything what Tiff had done to Jake. And she hated herself for agreeing to be a part of it.

For his own good, there were things he must never learn about Tiff, things that would only cause him further torment. Yet, the weight of guilt ate away at her resolve. How could she right the wrong he'd suffered? The pit in her stomach tightened.

If she could do nothing else to assuage her conscience, she must help Jake forge a strong relationship with Maisie. It was the least she could do. Was it, though?

Callie scrubbed her forehead. No matter how Jake's brokenness lashed her heart, Maisie had to be her top priority. But she would do what she could in helping Jake and Maisie find their way to each other.

She took a ragged breath. And then come November, he'd leave as they'd agreed. The idea of his departure left her with an unsettled feeling.

Later, upstairs in his bathroom, Jake splashed water on his face and examined the man he beheld in the mirror.

He hadn't anticipated the intense sense of loss he felt when he'd seen the photo of his newborn daughter in Tiffany's arms. It was pink-cheeked

Maisie that had made him emotional, not Tiffany, wasn't it?

Suddenly, he wasn't so sure. He'd believed himself over his ex-wife a long time ago. Only an idiot loved somebody who didn't love them back. Right?

He fingered the stubble on his jaw. Had he made a mistake in coming into Maisie's life? There were a lot of things worse than nothing. Such as having a father like his. Or Tiffany's.

In a way, it was that very dysfunction that had drawn them to each other. The problem was that neither of them had ever had a real home. No surprise they'd failed to make one with each other.

He sagged, bracing his hands on the sink. A lifetime of insecurity and self-doubt washed over him. What was he doing here, trying to be Maisie's father?

Jake had no business being anyone's father. The familiar childhood tape played over and over in his head. His dad's voice yelling it was Jake's fault his mother abandoned them.

Did it really even matter why Tiffany left? Had his dad been right about him being worthless? Perhaps Tiffany's desertion had answered that question once and for all.

He ought to leave Apple Valley Farm before he messed up Maisie as bad as his parents had messed up him. And yet…

Jake pictured the recent photo of Maisie's

happy face over her second birthday cake. Nash must've taken that picture. Lips pursed, Callie stood behind Maisie's chair, helping the little girl blow out her candles.

Per his agreement with Callie, he wouldn't be here to celebrate Maisie's third birthday or anything else. Perhaps if over the apple harvest Maisie learned to trust him again, he would be invited to return some day in the future. But he ached inside at how much he'd miss of his daughter's life.

The sound of laughter floated from outside. Straightening, he moved toward the bedroom window.

Almost ready to wink out behind the ridge, the sun cast a golden hue on two figures in the meadow. Against the glowing backdrop of sunset, Callie's hair seemed ablaze with a fiery light. She and the smaller form of Maisie waved.

His heart constricted. For a fraction of a second, he imagined they waved at him. His pulse ratcheted. An indescribable joy flooded over him.

The joy of mattering to someone. Of belonging to a family like the Jacksons, living and working in a beautiful place like the apple orchard. Having a woman like Callie love him.

He spotted Nash at the corner of the barn.

They were waving at Nash. The three of them—not him—belonged to each other. Tiffany's actions had made it crystal clear that, as he'd always suspected, there was something inside Jake that just wasn't lovable.

Arms outstretched, Maisie surged toward her beloved Pop-Pop. Callie followed a pace behind, her hand trailing through the petals of late-summer wildflowers. And despite not belonging—never belonging—Jake's heart caught in his throat. The sheer loveliness of her stirred something inside him.

Surrounded by the mountains, God felt very near to Jake, and casting aside the fear, hope bloomed for the first time in a long while in his heart. An answer to a prayer he'd been too afraid to voice.

Callie was his daughter's heart—he saw it clearly now—as truly as Maisie's heart belonged to Callie. With Callie's help, he might yet earn the love of his daughter.

And something else, too. He sensed that somehow he might've stumbled on to more than he had ever dreamed possible.

Home.

Chapter Four

Over the next few days, the busy Labor Day weekend proved to be a crash course for Jake in learning about apple farming. He pushed himself, working hard to prove to the Jacksons their trust in him wasn't misplaced.

In less than three months, harvest would be over and he'd be on his way to Houston. That was the deal with Callie, and he meant to abide by it. The Jackson farm was where Maisie belonged. In the meantime, he longed to form a relationship with his daughter.

Yet, despite Callie's attempts to soften Maisie's heart toward him, she hadn't thawed. Instead, his daughter's sky-blue eyes gazed at him with suspicion, and every day another piece of his hope died.

He didn't force her to interact with him, but he could feel her watching his every move. And if he accidentally got too close, she'd shrink into

Callie or Nash. She refused to let him touch her. She wouldn't talk to him.

But he wanted to know everything about her world, so in the empty years to come he could picture her life in his head. The people she'd grow up with. The town. Her little friends. Everything. It was all he'd ever have of her, and he meant to make the most of it.

So on Sunday, when Callie mentioned their routine included church, he asked to come, too. He could tell by the sudden light in Callie's eyes that his decision pleased her.

They rode together in Callie's sedan. With her father at the wheel, Callie insisted Jake ride shotgun in the front. Just as well. Maisie wouldn't want him sitting next to her in the back seat.

"We're always closed on Sunday mornings, but during apple season we open the store in the afternoon." Nash veered into the small graveled parking lot on the outskirts of town.

Nestled in a glade, the white-clapboard chapel made his heart skip a beat. The steeple brushed the picture-perfect autumn sky. After getting out of the car, he followed the Jacksons over the tiny footbridge spanning a small creek. Above the soft murmur of voices were sweet sounds of birdsong. He heard a sighing rustle in the color-splashed leaves and a burbling melody of rushing water over moss-covered stones.

Jake hung back as many of their friends called

out greetings. The Jacksons were well liked, and from the number of people stopping to speak to Maisie, she was a local favorite, too.

He'd made the right choice in not taking Maisie with him that first day. Maisie would have a good life in Truelove, surrounded by family and friends who would nurture and care for her. Unlike Jake's lonely childhood, Maisie's would have a supportive network to guide her growing-up years.

Maisie might even get married in this church one day. He stuck his hands in his pockets. Not that he'd be here to see it. Or be a part of one of the happiest days of her life.

But he was grateful to the Jacksons for this opportunity to know her, if even a little. And, as he wended his way into the sanctuary, he was grateful to God for bringing him here.

Callie carried Maisie into the foyer. "I need to drop Maisie off in the nursery, but I'll be back."

With her mouth pursed, Maisie glared at him over Callie's shoulder. Her hostility felt like a hundred barbed arrows in his chest. They disappeared through one of the doors flanking the pulpit.

Nash did his best to introduce Jake to friends from Truelove. At first, there were a few angry looks levied at him, but Nash was careful to set the record straight about how Jake had just found out about his daughter.

Assuring them that Maisie would continue living at Apple Valley Farm and that Jake was helping him with the harvest. Jake appreciated his efforts, recognizing it as Nash's attempt to give an outsider an insider seal of approval.

When the prelude music started, he and Nash took their places in one of the red-padded wooden pews. Peace permeated the chapel, and serenity—neither of which he'd had much experience with in his life.

"The church is over two hundred years old," Nash whispered. "Built by our Scots-Irish ancestors who came to the Appalachian Mountains on the Great Wagon Road before the American Revolution."

Huge hand-hewn beams soared above their heads. On the outside walls, stained-glass windows depicted Bible stories. Small brass plaques were mounted on the ends of pews. Many had the same family names as the people Nash had introduced him to earlier. A community of faith, a godly legacy and heritage. He was glad Maisie would have roots—something he'd never had.

Mountain worship was casual. He glanced around the rapidly filling sanctuary. Most of the men were in jeans or khakis and dress shirts. No ties or suits, which was good. Jake had only one outfit that wasn't jeans and work shirts—his army uniform. He'd put that life behind him for good in the hope of making a new life with his daughter, though that seemed a pipe dream now.

Jake observed Callie quietly as she emerged once again through the connecting door. She wore a filmy russet blouse over her brown wraparound skirt. As she moved toward them, her tawny hair captured the glow from the lit candles on the wooden altar.

He shifted for Callie to squeeze by him, but Nash scooted across the pew, leaving Callie no choice other than to sit between them.

Red splotches peppered her cheeks as she sank down beside Jake. And his stomach belly flopped as a scent of vanilla and cinnamon wafted past his nostrils in her wake.

A pucker formed in the bridge of her forehead. She bit her lip. Maisie wasn't the only one he unintentionally made uncomfortable. He wished he understood what it was he did or said that upset Callie. He'd promised her he wouldn't take Maisie, but maybe she didn't believe him or was afraid he'd change his mind.

More likely, she just didn't like him, influenced by what Tiffany had told her about him. There was probably nothing he could do to change Callie's opinion of him. Her feelings about him a foregone conclusion long before they ever met.

His stomach churned. If only he could somehow prove to Callie he could be trusted. Though why it mattered, he wasn't sure. In three months, he'd never see her again. Maisie, either.

Thereafter, his interactions with Callie would be confined to bank drafts for Maisie's needs, Christmas cards or a few emails with attached photos.

But Callie's discomfort in his presence bothered him. He liked and admired her, and the fact that she didn't feel the same about him saddened him.

At the front of the church, a young woman stepped onto the dais. She called out a page number, and a general fumbling for hymnbooks broke out in the pews around Jake.

There were two hymnals in the rack in their section. Nash's and Callie's hands grabbed for the same one. Nash jerked his chin in Jake's direction. Callie's eyes flashed. A brief tug-of-war ensued between her and her father for control of the hymnal.

Her father won. Nash proceeded to share the hymnal with a pretty woman about his age in hospital scrubs on his left.

That left only one hymnal remaining in the rack—one hymnal for his daughter and Jake to share. Stomach knotting, Jake stood next to Callie and chewed the inside of his cheek.

On the platform, the young woman lifted what Jake believed the people in Truelove would call a fiddle, tucking it under her chin. Drawing the bow across the string, she started the congregation on the first verse.

The tune was simple enough. The lilting quality of the song reminded him of the creek outside the church. Yet, he and Callie remained frozen in place.

An older lady across the aisle stopped singing, rubbernecking him and Callie. Craning their necks, two other women beside her also gawked. Bristling, Callie pushed the green-bound volume at Jake.

He shook his head. "I don't sing," he rasped.

Lips pressed tightly together, she thumbed through the pages until she found the right number. Without a word, she nudged the hymnal at him again.

The page fluttered. Her hand hung awkwardly between them, suspended in midair. Brows lowered, she just looked at him.

Hoping to alleviate the embarrassment he'd inadvertently caused, he hefted his share of the hymnal in his hand. She skimmed the words, and with her index finger, she pointed to a line in the second verse.

So what else could he do? The melody wasn't hard. The music flowed over him.

But to read the words, he was forced to stand even closer to Callie. It made his pulse race to be so near her. His breath caught. His heart hammered.

Their sleeves touching, he was surprised—

agreeably so—when she didn't shift away. Maybe she was getting not to mind him so much?

Like most of the people singing with gusto all around him, she didn't seem to need the words. Singing in a strong, clear contralto, she hardly glanced at the page.

The stirring words about love and mercy reflected in her brown eyes and on the faces of the other worshippers. He wasn't sure what to make of the church and these people. Until Callie had surprised him by asking him to stay for a while, he'd experienced little of either love or mercy in his life.

A while, the part he couldn't afford to forget. He strengthened his grip on the hymnal. This wasn't meant to last forever. Nothing good ever did.

The lady fiddler ended the song with a final flourish of her bow. The last note hung high and clear, quivering with sudden stillness in the rafters above their heads.

Taking the book out of his hands, Callie replaced it in the rack, and following her lead, he sat down.

When the reverend Bryant called the congregation to pray, Jake glanced around at the bowed heads before bending his own. Blond, brown, gray and variations on a theme of red. He bit off a smile, thinking of Callie. A lot of red was sprinkled throughout the mountain congregation.

Shutting his eyes, Jake allowed the pastor's words of peace to wash over him. Reverend Bryant talked to God like He was right there beside him, like talking to a friend. As natural as breathing, Nash and Callie did the same when they said a prayer of blessing over mealtimes.

Was God really that close? Close enough to hear? Or was that kind of relationship reserved for good people like the Jacksons? Like the people in the pews?

Could God ever want to hear from somebody like him? Jake gulped past the mountain-size knot in his throat as the pastor ended the prayer.

The sermon wasn't what Jake expected or wanted to hear.

Reverend Bryant gripped both sides of the pulpit. "Forgive as you want to be forgiven."

He settled his shoulders against the pew, folding his arms across his chest. Forgive his brutal father for a miserable childhood? Forgive the one person who was supposed to love him the most—his mother—for abandoning him? For leaving him behind? For betraying him?

Unfolding his arms, he fisted his hands beside his legs on the pew. Not likely he'd forgive what Tiffany had done—robbing Jake of a future with his daughter.

If God expected him to forgive his so-called wife for walking out on him and taking his child with her, God and he weren't ever likely to get any better acquainted.

All that forgiveness talk might be fine for the mountain people in Truelove. But what did any of them know about what he'd gone through, what he'd suffered? Let them talk about forgiveness when they'd been through what he'd endured.

He unfisted his hands. Yet, Callie had forgiven Jake and given him a second chance. He knew Christian people set a great store on forgiveness, but where Jake had come from, forgiveness was almost an alien concept.

Still, was that where he needed to start if he had any hope of putting his life back together? Forgiving Tiffany. *Seriously, God?*

Leaning forward, he rested his elbows on his thighs and laced his hands together. What about the rest of his life post-Maisie? After November, once again Jake would have no one.

Except for God. A startling realization. God might prove to be the one being Jake could take with him. The one being who would never leave Jake.

If—a big if—he could trust God not to let him down the way everyone else in Jake's existence had. He'd think more on this forgiveness stuff later. Sort through the confusing tangle of emotions within himself that he didn't understand.

When the preacher called the congregation to sing the final hymn, lost in thought, it took Jake a second longer than the rest of the church to respond. He scrambled to his feet.

"Here." Callie thrust his half of the hymnbook at him.

Jake reddened.

At the final "Amen" she pushed past him, stumbling into the aisle, leaving him and the hymnal hanging. Making it as plain as an apple-crisp mountain day, that Callie Jackson could barely tolerate his presence.

Like his mother. Like Tiffany. Like God?

Proving once again how easy he was to walk away from.

She'd made a right fool of herself, tumbling out of the pew and staggering down the aisle. She had to get to Maisie, to safety.

Her cheeks felt on fire as she hurried toward the nursery.

But standing so close to Jake McAbee... breathing in the clean, woodsy scent of him. Despite what he'd said, his voice was a pleasing if rusty baritone, rising alongside hers. Blending together as if one, as if right where he...she... *they* belonged.

Her heart whispered that she needed to tell him the truth, but she couldn't do that. Revealing Tiff's secret—what she'd asked Callie to never tell Jake—would bring dire consequences.

She practically ran down the church corridor, running from self-recrimination and one incontrovertible truth. Her insistence on keeping Maisie close to her heart was breaking Jake McAbee's. Even worse, God's, too?

Approaching the nursery, she came to an abrupt halt. With her hand to her throat, she pressed her shoulder blades against the smoothness of the wall. She had to stop this. Stop second-guessing herself. Stop this rush of tenderness toward Maisie's father.

She squeezed her eyes shut.

Every time she got within ten feet of the rugged ex-soldier, her feelings became as tangled as kudzu. He confused her, flustered her, derailed her from her original purpose.

Jake McAbee made her feel things she'd believed she'd never feel. Feelings that belonged to other people. Not for someone with a child to raise and an apple orchard to run. Impossible feelings for someone keeping secrets.

And yet, when he looked at her…

Swallowing, she poked her head into the nursery.

Catching sight of Callie through the open half door, Maisie's face lit up. "Cawee!" Knocking over the pile of blocks, Maisie scrambled to her feet.

Her heart quickened with a torrent of nearly overwhelming love. She must put aside these nagging doubts and take the long perspective.

She was doing the right thing for Maisie, for all of them.

Wasn't she?

"Hey, sweetie pie." Maneuvering through the childproof lock on the doorknob, she swept the little girl into her arms. "Thank you!" she called out to the married couple on nursery duty today.

"Wunch?"

Striding out the side entrance of the church, Callie repositioned Maisie on her hip. She couldn't bear to think of the day when Maisie would get too heavy for her to carry. But now that Maisie was potty trained, at least there were no more diaper bags to tote.

Callie hurried down the wooden ramp. "We'll have lunch soon as we get home, sweet girl. Then a nap." The teenagers she hired on the weekends would man the store.

Maisie scowled. "No cwib. Big-gull bed. No nap May-zee."

Sighing, she readjusted Maisie's weight. "But BooWoo is probably tired, don't you think?"

Maisie's gaze lifted. "BooWoo?"

The suede, gray-striped stuffed tabby cat Maisie had been attached to since infancy.

Callie tilted her head. "Maybe you could help BooWoo fall asleep?"

Maisie nodded. "Big-gull hep." She jabbed her thumb into her chest.

Callie smiled. "That's right. You are a big

girl. My snuggly, wuggly big girl." She tickled Maisie's tummy.

But rounding the corner of the church, Callie came to a complete standstill. Jake was encircled by the Truelove matchmakers, the entire posse of them.

The sixtysomething ladies were notorious for poking their powdered noses where they didn't belong. For years, they'd been after Callie's dad to remarry, throwing one eligible, matchmaker-vetted widow or divorcée after the other at him.

And some help her father was proving to be. On the other side of the footbridge, her dad was talking to Lorena. She was their closest farm neighbor. Wearing her nurse scrubs, she was either coming off a shift or starting one at the regional medical center.

There'd be no help for Jake there. Or for Callie, either. The Truelove matchmakers were tougher than they looked. With the ladies blocking access to the bridge—the only escape route—there was no avoiding them.

Might as well face the issue head-on. Truelove was a small town and, like most small towns, possessed a formidable grapevine, faster by far than any text message. The ladies would be wanting to meet Maisie's father.

These ladies had been good to Callie's mother during her long illness, and to Callie and her father ever since.

Stepping forward, she squared her shoulders. "Miss IdaLee. Miss GeorgeAnne. Miss Erma-Jean."

Not unlike a deer caught in the glare of on-coming headlights, Jake's eyes darted around the cluster of women.

Married, divorced or spinster, the "Miss" was an honorary title of respect bestowed on any Southern lady who was your elder in age. No matter if the "Miss" was elderly or not.

"Why, CallieRose—" the uncontested leader of the pack, GeorgeAnne, said Callie's name like she did her own, the words running together "—do introduce us to this handsome young man."

Jake flushed. It was all Callie could do not to laugh, but she took pity on him and came to his rescue.

"ErmaJean Hicks, IdaLee Moore, GeorgeAnne Allen, I'd like you to meet Jake McAbee."

"Ma'am." He inclined his head at each in turn. "ErmaJean. IdaLee. GeorgeAnne?" He blinked. "Such…unusual—I mean, I don't think I've ever heard such lovely names before."

Jake McAbee was quick on the draw. She'd give him that. Maybe he hadn't needed her help after all.

"How nice." Miss ErmaJean fluttered her lashes. "Such a gentleman."

Jake's eyes cut to Callie's. Again, she suppressed the urge to laugh. But en masse, the

Truelove matchmakers could be a bit over-whelming. More than a bit.

Callie rubbed Maisie's back. "The ladies are founding members of Truelove's Double Name Club." She stuck her tongue in her cheek. "An old and beloved tradition among Southern families."

"And it goes so well with the drawl, too." Jake gave her a slow, lazy grin.

Her knees suddenly wobbly, she gaped at him, and that discombobulated, tingly sensation every time she was near him started again. When he smiled at her like that… She gulped. Jake McAbee ought to come with warning labels.

Callie became aware that the ladies had gone still, their eyes behind wire-rimmed frames large and sharp. Not unlike a cat zeroing in on a mouse. Somehow she'd momentarily forgotten about them, which was never a good thing when dealing with the matchmakers.

They could get an entirely wrong idea about what was between her and Jake. *Was* there something between her and Jake? Her heart thumped.

"Such a cute family you make." Subtlety wasn't GeorgeAnne's strong suit.

Callie felt the heat crawling up her neck. Before she could frame an appropriate response, Miss IdaLee, the oldest of Truelove's matriarchs, laid her slightly gnarled, blue-veined hand gently on Maisie's blond head.

"Isn't it wonderful to have your papa with you at long last, Maisie honey?"

Callie hadn't imagined that two-year-olds were capable of curling their lip.

Maisie drew herself up and with great deliberation stared fixedly at the surrounding glade of trees. Anywhere and everywhere but at her father.

Callie's heart fell to her toes. Her gaze cut to Jake, hoping, praying, he hadn't seen Maisie's reaction—but he had. As had the ladies. His Adam's apple bobbed.

At the look on his face, she wanted to weep for him. He dropped his eyes to the grass. Not thinking, she took a step closer, reaching out to him.

The gesture was not lost on the matchmakers. Becoming aware of how such a gesture could be misinterpreted, she let her hand fall.

"Our Maisie and her father will get used to each other." GeorgeAnne cleared her throat. "Nothing that a little time won't heal."

"Will it?" Jake whispered as if to himself. "Does time heal all wounds?"

GeorgeAnne's glacier-blue gaze softened. "With the Lord's help, I believe it can." She gave his shoulder a quick pat. "Hang in there."

Callie warmed toward the often sharp-tongued, overly brusque woman.

Excited shouts broke out. "Maisie! Maisie!"

Callie's good friend, Amber, waved. Amber's

two energetic girls rushed over, breaking the moment. The twins proved enough to send the matchmakers into a temporary retreat.

The ladies moved across the footbridge toward their vehicles, but Callie had an uncomfortable feeling neither she nor Jake had heard the last of the matchmakers.

Although a few years older, Amber's girls were Maisie's best friends, too. Long ago during high school, she dated Amber's brother, hoping one day to call Amber a sister. But that wasn't meant to be.

Callie set Maisie on her feet to chat with her little friends, but she kept a firm grip on her hand.

Perhaps Jake had had about as much female companionship as he could tolerate, because he slipped across the bridge as Amber drew closer.

"You can thank me later," Amber laughed, watching the matchmakers disperse to their cars.

"Not soon enough." Callie rolled her eyes. "But I owe you. Free babysitting any night of your choice. What's your class schedule like this week?"

"You don't have to do that." Amber shook her head. "You always look after my girls for free."

"Because I love doing it. It's no bother."

Amber gave Callie a little hip bump. "Nice try, changing the subject. But you're not getting off the hook so easily. Not until you bring Maisie's dad into the diner and introduce me to this man who has you so rattled."

"He does not." Dropping her hold on Maisie, she crossed her arms and then uncrossed them. "I am not."

"Uh-huh."

"Jake… It isn't…" She smoothed her skirt. "I have no idea what you're talking about."

Amber's lips twitched. "Uh-huh."

"Stop saying that." Callie took hold of Maisie's shoulder, preventing her from sliding into the small creek bed. "He does not."

Catching hold of the slippery-as-eel twins, Amber led them across the footbridge. She threw Callie a parting shot. "Sure about that?"

Actually, when it came to Jake McAbee, Callie wasn't sure about anything.

Chapter Five

Callie said nothing more to Jake about the incident with the Truelove matchmakers at church. But that afternoon, when she got her father alone in the barn, she gave him an earful about his failure to protect one of his own—an unattached male—from the clutches of the infamous matchmakers.

It was Jake himself, however, who broached the subject a few days later when he came into the house. "About those ladies…" At the kitchen sink, he cranked the faucet, letting the cool water flow over his muscled forearms.

She didn't have to ask which ladies. "I'll help you sort them out individually by name, so next time you won't feel so ambushed."

He lathered the bar of soap, scrubbing his hands and his forearms beneath his rolled-up sleeves. "Culling the herd?" He rolled his tongue in his cheek. "Divide and conquer?"

She laughed. Jake McAbee could always make her laugh. She hadn't expected that when she first met him. And she appreciated his easygoing manner in the aftermath of what had to have been an unspeakable embarrassment for him on Sunday.

"Consider it a survival mechanism for living in Truelove." She handed him a towel. "I'm sorry that it happened at all."

He rubbed his arms with the towel so vigorously she feared he'd scrub off his skin. "No one's fault, except mine."

She wished he weren't always so quick to take the blame for everything.

"What the ladies said about you, me, Maisie…" Callie fidgeted. "They feel it's their duty…" This wasn't coming out right. "They take our town motto a little too seriously…"

He spread the towel over the counter to dry. "Truelove, where true love awaits."

Maybe this would come out easier if she didn't have to look at him. The tic jumping in his cheek was distracting, as was the tanned skin on his throat above the open collar of his denim shirt.

She stirred the soup pot on the stove. "Any eligible bachelor is fair game, I'm afraid."

Jake leaned his hip against the kitchen island. "I'm sorry they embarrassed you. You deserve far better than to be publicly linked to someone like me. Next time I see them, I'll set the record straight."

There he went again.

Gripping the spoon, she spun around. "That's not what I meant."

"You're dripping."

She frowned. "What?"

He pointed to the tomato sauce dribbling off the spoon in her hand.

"Oh…" After grabbing the cloth on the counter, she bent over the kitchen floor.

Ripping a paper towel off the rod, Jake also crouched. And *smack*, their foreheads collided, knocking both of them onto their keisters.

She fell against the under-sink cabinet. "Ow!"

Grunting, Jake landed against the island cabinet door, but humor danced in his blue eyes. "You've got a hard head, farm girl."

Forgetting she still clutched the wooden spoon, she moved to rub her brow and succeeded only in braining herself with the utensil, thoroughly splattering sauce all over the floor. She groaned.

"Callie…"

She liked how he said her name, how the syllables rumbled from his chest, rolled from between his lips. With her eyes, she traced the line from his stubble-covered jaw to his mouth.

"Callie…"

Her gaze lifted to meet his. "W-what?" she gasped, a breathy note in her voice.

"You're wearing the sauce now."

"I—I am?"

He gave her a crooked smile. "You are."

She dropped the spoon with a clatter. "Where?" She swiped at her forehead. "Here? Is that better?"

He leaned forward on his knees. "And here." Taking her chin between his thumb and forefinger, he wiped away a streak of tomato sauce.

The butterflies in her chest went into full flight mode. A quick intake of breath brought his woodsy scent to her nostrils.

Cupping her cheek in his palm, his thumb gently moved across her cheek. "Better now." His voice sounded hoarse.

"Much better," she whispered, lost in the intensity of his gaze.

"Cawee!" Maisie barked.

Jolting, she and Jake sprang apart.

Hands propped on her little hips, Maisie glared at her—not Jake—as if Callie had consorted with the enemy and betrayed Maisie's trust.

Callie's heart hammered. "Maisie, you scared me."

How long had she been standing there? Not that anything had happened. What would have happened, though, if Maisie hadn't interrupted?

She flushed.

Jumping up, Jake started to offer his hand to help Callie stand. But when Maisie transferred her scowl to him, he stuffed his hands into his pockets.

She jabbed her tiny finger at Jake. "No wike him, Cawee."

He flinched. "I'll call Nash to the table." Dropping his eyes, he lumbered toward the screen porch. The door slammed behind him, settling into the frame with a dull thud.

She'd promised herself she wouldn't scold Maisie for her feelings about her father or her lack of feeling. But even if only two years old, Maisie's uncharacteristic rudeness couldn't be allowed to go unchecked.

Catching hold of the edge of the counter, she leveraged herself upright. "I don't like your attitude, Maisie Nicole McAbee. Nor the way you treat your daddy."

Maisie's eyes—so like Jake's?—narrowed at Callie.

"We talked about how your daddy didn't mean to scare you that first day. He would never hurt you. You don't need to be afraid." Callie smoothed her blouse. "He's trying so hard. I don't understand why you are so mean to him. He loves you so much."

Maisie's blond curls flew as she shook her head from side to side. "No May-zee daddy. No wike."

"If you'd only give him a chance." She went down to Maisie's level. "Please?"

Giving Callie a nice view of her back, Maisie returned to her toys in the living room. Her feelings in regard to her father were only too clear. Her attitude, intractable.

Callie rocked on her heels. Maisie gave new definition to *stubborn*. A trait Maisie's mother, Tiff, had possessed in spades. The "cutting off your nose to spite your face" kind of stubbornness. A stubbornness that too often had resulted in disaster for Tiff.

Like mother, like daughter? *God, please, no.* Not when she was doing everything in her power to make sure Maisie never went down the road Tiff had chosen.

Standing beside the island, she watched Maisie play with her plastic barn animals. Love welled inside Callie for this child who'd grown not under her heart, but in it.

That had to count for something. *Doesn't it, God?* Love had been the essential ingredient Tiff's childhood had lacked. The seed from which so many of Tiff's bad choices had sprung.

Callie had tried loving Tiff through her mistakes, but in the end, Tiff had left only carnage in her wake. Wrecking her own life. Devastating other lives, like Jake's.

She wanted so much more for Maisie. But what counted for more? Despite everything Callie had done, was a child's future determined more by heredity than environment? If that was true—and this was what she feared most—then Maisie's parental genes potentially meant a lifetime of unhappiness and ruin.

All of the fight went out of Callie. She slumped against the edge of the counter, hope draining from her like water through a sieve.

The screen door squeaked as her father tromped inside the house. Maisie scrambled to her feet, and her Pop-Pop swept her into a bear hug.

When he entered quietly, Jake's emotional exhaustion hit her like a visceral blow. The hopelessness of ever reclaiming his daughter's affection was etched across his shadowed face.

She couldn't—mustn't—let Jake accept defeat. He was key to making sure what happened to Tiff never happened to Maisie. Biting her lip, she pivoted toward the stove.

If she could just figure out a way to get the both of them over this initial hurdle and jump-start a real relationship between them, for the sake of Maisie's future happiness. She ladled the sauce over the pasta on each of the four blue pottery plates.

Callie's dad toted Maisie off to the downstairs half bath to wash her hands for dinner.

Without being asked, Jake removed the silverware from the drawer and set the table. Always working hard to "earn" a place at the table.

She hadn't expected Jake McAbee to tug at her heart so much.

Maisie was too young to understand, but she needed a father in her life.

Callie worried her lip between her teeth. A long-distance father? That was the "arrangement" she'd made with Jake. But what else was she supposed to do? She carried her father's plate to the table.

Maisie belonged on the farm, not with a man she barely knew. A man with no home and no real roots. What kind of example would that be to Maisie?

Jake carried over the other two plates, placing one on her place mat and the other on Maisie's. He left himself for last, like always.

Callie's heart wrenched. Grabbing a glass, she pressed it against the lever on the ice dispenser at the fridge. Ice cubes plonked into it.

Tiff had made it clear she wanted Callie to raise her child, which was the reason Callie fought to keep Maisie here. This wasn't about her needs or the hole Maisie filled in her life. She was honoring Tiff's wishes. Right?

Jake rushed over. "Callie, let me help."

She blinked at him. "Help?" What did he mean?

He gestured toward the overflowing glass. Still-falling ice cubes littered the kitchen floor.

"Oh... I'm..." Biting her lip, she stopped pressing the glass against the lever. "Thanks."

"Callie Girl, is everything all right?" Standing behind the chair, her father had already settled Maisie into her booster seat. Both of them stared at the skating rink she'd created in the kitchen.

"I—I..." She waved her arms, sloshing additional ice cubes out of the glass and onto the floor. "I got distracted."

Jake took the glass from her. "Go sit down. I'll clean this up for you."

Shouldn't she clean up her own messes? Wasn't that what she was doing, and doing so badly? Trying to clean up Tiff's mess?

"Callie." Her father pulled out her chair. "Take a break, sweetheart."

So she sat. While Jake, good guy that he was—despite her desire to believe otherwise—scooped up each errant ice cube. He and her father made sure to mop any wet spots on the floor. Stuffed cat clutched in her arms, Maisie entertained herself by talking in the singsong little voice she used with BooWoo, her beloved companion.

Callie's heart drummed in her chest. Why was she so determined to find fault with Jake? To ease her own conscience? To justify keeping Maisie from him?

Tying Maisie's plastic bib behind her neck, Callie's father finished with a quick peck on her cheek. Maisie giggled. Jake tried to keep his face expressionless—a defense mechanism?—

but Maisie's affection for Pop-Pop, in contrast to how she felt about her own father, must tear him apart inside. Bringing the other glasses to the table, Jake sat down.

Meals must be both a joy and a tremendous sorrow for him, she realized. Maybe all of this was for naught anyway. Maybe she should just—

She gave herself a shake.

If she came clean with her doubts, he might walk away from Maisie for good, which was not something she was willing to risk. There were other factors to consider.

She'd promised to always keep Maisie safe. Her "deal" with Jake seemed the only way to ensure that. Though like the deal she'd made with Tiff, she was starting to get sick of that word.

Callie's father cleared his throat. "Let's thank God for this wonderful meal."

Maisie steepled her small hands.

Callie took a deep breath. She had to stay the course. History would not repeat itself—not while she had breath in her body.

Because the alternative…? Her appetite suddenly gone, she cut her eyes to Jake's bowed head. The alternative—that Jake would never again be a part of their lives—was unthinkable.

Chapter Six

With apple season well underway, Jake worked from dawn till dusk every day. Actually, later than that, because each evening he and Nash returned to the shed beside the cooler to grade the newly picked apples to sell at the store the next day.

September had come and gone, and he'd learned a lot about the orchard business. Ninety percent of Nash's crop was sold retail to the general public. Harvest months from Labor Day to mid-November were crucial in earning their yearly income and keeping the orchard afloat financially. Only 10 percent of the crop was sold to wholesalers to be processed into applesauce, cider or baby food.

There were much larger orchards around True-love, but this was a family-owned, family-run operation. And Nash liked it that way. Jake, too. The Jacksons had as much business as they could handle—enough to keep them on the land their ancestors had farmed for centuries.

It surprised Jake how much he enjoyed the slower pace of life in the country. The satisfying connection he felt to the soil. The joy of working with his hands.

Despite his rough childhood, combat and Tiffany, he was a simple man. Or perhaps it was because of those things that he had simple tastes.

Simple pleasures. Easily pleased for the most part. It didn't take much. He'd learned to never expect much. Safer that way. Less disillusionment.

Up with the birds each morning, Jake didn't mind. Callie made sure no one went hungry. He'd never worked harder; he'd never been happier.

Except for Maisie's continuing hostility.

But he couldn't dwell on that. Like a plow horse, he just did the work in front of him that day—mowing the rows between the trees, fixing equipment. Whatever the orchard required. Jake liked how each day's challenges were different.

Nash taught him how to tell when the apples were ready to be harvested. Climbing the narrow-at-the-top tripod ladder leaning against a tree, Jake would place apple after apple into the pick bag as he worked.

The army had seen he kept fit, but after climbing ladders all day, he'd discovered muscles—sore muscles—he'd never known he had.

"Preschool group due 'bout ten this morning." Nash adjusted the brim of his John Deere ball cap. "A perfect day to visit the orchard."

Every day, in Jake's opinion, was a perfect day to be at the orchard. But he knew what Nash meant. Mornings now possessed an apple-crunch crispness. The early-October sun still warmed the afternoons, but by nightfall the mountain air bathed the orchard valley with a cold clarity.

Jake stepped off the last rung of the aluminum ladder onto the ground. "The tractor and the wagon are ready to go." With the padded strap of the pick bag slung over his shoulder, he strode toward the wooden bin.

He and Nash had already been working for a few hours. Callie, too. First, dropping off Maisie to two-year-old preschool and then getting the kitchen at the Apple House ready for customers.

Gently—like Nash had taught him—Jake unloaded the bag of apples into the bin so as not to bruise them.

"Where most of the apples are lost," Nash had told him early in the harvest. "Can't sell them to the public then. Good for nothing but pie."

Power of suggestion?

Catching a whiff of baked apples, Jake straightened. He shaded his hand over his eyes. In every direction, leafed out, heavily laden apple trees covered the orchard. Over the hill near the road lay the shed, the cooler building and the

Apple House with its tantalizing scents. Behind Jake, over another hill, stood the meadow, house and barn.

Hand in his overalls pocket, Nash jingled his keys. "That's it for this load."

Jake's stomach rumbled.

Nash grinned. "The ladies at the Apple House will be glad to get you a snack before the ankle biters arrive. I'll be there myself directly."

Jake lifted the strap over his head and off his shoulder. "I'll go fat with all the food those ladies push at me."

Nash headed toward the forklift. "No chance of that." He winked as he climbed aboard the tractor. "Working you too hard for that to happen."

"I'm not complaining," Jake called up to him.

Nash reached over to switch on the engine. "Best worker I've ever had. I've got no complaints about you, son."

Son. Not something Jake had ever been called before. The names he'd been called had usually come in the aftermath of a fist to the face. But if he could've selected a father for himself, someone like Nash Jackson would've topped the list.

Nash rolled the tractor forward. The tines of the forklift caught the wooden pallet beneath the bin, hoisting it into the air. With a shift of gears, the tractor lurched away toward the cooler.

Jake would sort the bin tonight. Unless, of

course, the store ran out of apples. Then he would find himself doing a quick grading to restock the crates.

Pink Ladies, Nash called the variety on this particular row of trees. "Best eating apples," Nash had said. "In my humble, but expert, opinion."

Speaking of eating? His stomach making itself felt again, Jake headed toward the rise. The exercise would do him good.

Right before he consumed yet another apple cider doughnut. Or three. He smiled, enjoying the sunshine on his face.

The parking lot was semifull, with more vehicles pulling off the secondary road. Across the road the blue smoke, for which the Blue Ridge was aptly named, hung over the mountain.

He slipped through the back door of the Apple House. Filled with mouthwatering aromas, the commercial kitchen bustled with local women. The seasonal baking crew worked morning or afternoon shifts, helping the Jacksons during apple season. As he'd discovered, it did take a village to work apple season.

"Jake."

He scraped his boots on the mat. "Miss GeorgeAnne."

GeorgeAnne Allen owned the hardware store in town. With her tall, solid frame and short-cropped iron-gray hair, she could hold her own in any discussion involving farming. And for some inexplicable reason, she'd taken a shine to him—Nash's observation.

Jake wasn't sure whether that was a good thing or not.

Miss GeorgeAnne lifted the rack of fried doughnuts out of the vat. "Saved you some from the previous batch. Not so hot as these. Ready to eat."

Gruff as usual, she nudged her squared-off jaw toward the stainless-steel table. Reverend Bryant's wife was boxing cinnamon-powdered doughnuts for a customer waiting beyond the open partition at the front counter.

His lips twitched. "Going like hotcakes, I mean, doughnuts, huh?"

Miss GeorgeAnne quirked an eyebrow, her lips pursing in what Jake had come to believe passed for a smile.

He shuffled over, snagging two doughnuts. "I appreciate you looking out for me, Miss GeorgeAnne." He bit into a doughnut and closed his eyes, savoring the flavors on his tongue.

"Apple, cinnamon and brown sugar…" She handed him a napkin.

He wiped his mouth, feeling like a schoolkid. But it wasn't just him. The matchmaker ladies, he'd noticed, had that effect on everyone.

"What home should taste like."

He looked away toward the front of the store,

unable to meet her gaze. "Yes, ma'am." Though, until he came to Apple Valley Farm, this was not something he'd understood.

She checked the oven, watching the pies bake through the glass-fronted door and giving him time to recover himself. Not overly given to sentiment herself, Miss GeorgeAnne was good about stuff like that.

Though semiretired, GeorgeAnne drove her family crazy at the hardware store in Truelove, according to Callie. And—Callie's lips had twitched when she told him—GeorgeAnne's family reckoned the Jacksons were doing them a favor by allowing her to work over here five mornings a week for the duration of harvest.

Jake polished off the last doughnut and under her eagle-eyed scrutiny made sure he wiped his hands. "Callie gone to drop off Maisie?"

Her mouth puckering, Miss GeorgeAnne's focus strayed to one of the new ladies who wasn't rolling the batch of doughnuts to her satisfaction. GeorgeAnne ran a tight ship.

"Out front." She waved him off. "Take a few more to tide you over till lunch." GeorgeAnne marched forward to harangue the hapless church lady. He'd been dismissed.

Taking her at her word, he grabbed a couple more doughnuts and ventured into the public area of the store.

Never-met-a-stranger ErmaJean rang up a customer's order. "We're open daily this time of year from eight thirty to six. On Sundays, though, we open at one."

Coffee burbled in the pot on the warmer. There were apple fritters in the display case, and bagged fresh loaves of pumpkin and apple bread on the shelves. On ice, cider jugs were encased in the large aluminum tub. Hay bales, scarecrows and fake autumn leaf garlands galore ensured no one forgot the season. But no Callie.

Miss ErmaJean Hicks, as apple round as GeorgeAnne was spare, sidled over to Jake. "So wonderful the way you're helping the Jacksons since Nash isn't quite himself yet."

Jake edged toward the entrance.

"Such an asset you'd be—long-term—" he inched closer to escape "—as a son-in-law—"

Nearly there...

Maybe Callie was outside helping customers select apples from the raised green-painted wooden stand. Yep. He eased out onto the open-fronted market, content to watch her for a moment. With that lovely auburn hair of hers, it never took more than a second for his eyes to pick her out of a crowd.

She didn't see him leaning against the door frame, eating another doughnut. He really needed to get a handle on eating doughnuts, though over the course of a day he more than worked it off.

Only a temporary problem, since he would be moving on after harvest season.

He grimaced. It was not a thought that brought comfort, almost putting him off his appetite for the final bite. But that didn't stop him from popping the last bite into his mouth. Okay, no more today. Who was he kidding? Tomorrow he'd just switch to the fritters.

"Granny Smiths make the best pies." Callie placed the last apple into the white bag. She handed the peck of apples to the young couple. "But while you're driving the parkway, you might want to buy a pie to take to your rental cabin."

The young man grinned. "Or two."

Leaf peepers. That was what locals called the tourists who arrived in droves this time of year to see the colorful display of autumnal splendor from the Blue Ridge Parkway vistas.

"Right through the door, Miss ErmaJean will get you those pies." For the first time, she noticed Jake standing there.

Blushing, her smile faltered, but she was an old hand at closing a deal. "Take some cider with you, too. Squeezed fresh. Tall glass, frosted with ice chips? Thirst-quenching. Best beverage in the world."

He moved aside to let the couple pass through. Skittish as a barnyard cat, Callie shifted around to the other side of the crate. Callie Jackson confused him.

Sometimes she acted like they could be the best of friends, and then other times like she couldn't stand to be around him. He wished she didn't dislike him so much.

Callie rearranged a row of Fuji apples and rearranged them some more. A methodical, if manic, orchard version of the shell game.

"You got Maisie off to preschool, I guess?"

Wrong question.

Her chin came up. "If you're implying that I'm farming her out—"

Palms raised, he retreated a step. "I wasn't—"

"Because this is the first year we've ever sent her to the church program." Her eyes flashed. "Only two mornings a week. Because it gets so busy here this time of year."

"You're run off your feet."

She folded her arms across her beige cable-knit sweater. "It's a safety hazard. Maisie could get hurt around the hot kitchen equipment. It gives me two mornings a week to at least make sure the Apple House is running smoothly. It wasn't so hard before when she was smaller, but now…"

"Now Maisie's a big girl and harder to contain. I understand, Callie." He took a tentative step in her direction. "It's no big deal."

She glared at him another moment as if she wasn't sure he wasn't going to yet criticize her parenting skills. When he didn't say anything, she deflated a notch. "And I worried Maisie wasn't getting enough interaction with other children out here on the farm with only the trees and bluebirds for company."

He cocked his head. "Don't forget BooWoo."

She laughed before she caught herself, and she let her defensive posture drop. "Right." Maisie wouldn't sleep without her little stuffed cat.

He smiled.

Grin fading, Callie backed away from him. Somehow he'd managed to put his foot in it again. They both turned as a caravan of vehicles pulled in to the lot.

She put more distance between them. "The preschoolers are here."

His gut clenched. She really disliked him.

An assortment of women and kids piled out of the SUVs.

"I guess I'm on." He lifted his ball cap, swiping his arm across his forehead before settling it again on his head.

A vein in the hollow of her throat jumping, Callie stared at him.

"What?"

She startled. "Nothing." She played with the tiny gold apple dangling from a chain around her neck.

"Do I have dirt on my face? Or just afraid my ugly mug will scare the kids?"

"Your face isn't..." She traced the toe of her

sneaker in the gravel. "Not at all, I mean…" She wiped her hands down the sides of her jeans. "Your hair."

He frowned. "What about my hair?"

"It's growing out—" She clamped her lips shut. "Oh, look who's here for her first big-girl field trip." Eyes wide, Callie hurtled past him.

Miss IdaLee and his daughter emerged from a silver sedan.

"Cawee!" Maisie rushed forward to embrace Callie's knees.

Sometimes it hurt Jake to look at his daughter. To see how exuberant her love was for everyone but him. Perhaps the same thing occurred to Callie, because she glanced over to him, her eyes flickering.

He cleared his throat. "I didn't realize it was Maisie's class scheduled for the orchard tour today." He inclined his head toward IdaLee. "Ma'am."

IdaLee Moore, he'd learned, was the oldest of the Truelove matchmakers. Very petite. But he'd not realized she was also Maisie's preschool teacher.

As if reading his mind, Callie brought Maisie over to him. "On Tuesdays and Thursdays, Miss IdaLee works afternoons at the Apple House. So she brings Maisie home from school, saving us a trip to town."

Maisie pretended he wasn't there. A skill she'd taken to an art form.

"Little early today." In her sensible black teacher shoes and wool skirt, IdaLee glided after them. "Taught most of the county in either Sunday school or elementary school before I retired."

White hair glinting in the sun, she patted Maisie's back. With her head tucked into Callie's shoulder, Maisie smiled shyly at her teacher.

Jake tried not to wince at yet another reminder that Maisie was okay with everyone in the universe touching her; everyone except him.

Miss IdaLee wasn't as fragile as she looked, however. In the blink of an eye, she had the rest of her charges corralled with detailed instructions about her expectations for behavior. And she wasn't only talking to the children. Callie set Maisie on her feet.

With the moms properly subdued, IdaLee cast a critical eye over her ragtag group of two-year-olds exclaiming over the red, green and yellow apples in the bins. "It'll take all of us to oversee this crowd."

She angled to Jake. "You may ready the wagon. We'll meet you momentarily." Her attention snapped to one of the moms. "Lacey Miller, once upon an apple, I seem to remember having a word with you about that very same thing…" Her bony finger pointed at the little boy scooping handfuls of gravel into his fists.

The mother scurried over to control her son. The army could've learned a thing or two from Miss IdaLee. Jake wiped the smile off his face before IdaLee turned on him. A scuffle broke out between two children at the stand.

Callie threw him a desperate glance. *Please, take me with you*, she mouthed over Miss Ida-Lee's diminutive head.

But laughing—quietly—he got out while the getting was good.

Getting the hayride ready for them, Jake watched the proceedings, gratefully, from afar. He liked kids, but in smaller numbers. To his reckoning, a dozen at once qualified as a baptism by fire.

Miss IdaLee led her platoon around to the hay wagon Jake had attached to the tractor. Not Callie, though. She returned to the Apple House. Technically, Maisie was under Miss IdaLee's charge for a couple more hours.

IdaLee could have single-handedly run the Normandy invasion. Jake stuck his tongue in his cheek. Who knows? At her age, perhaps she had.

His daughter's eyes lit at the sight of the purring green tractor. Such a farm girl.

Jake helped the moms and their children climb into the straw-filled wagon. But when it was Maisie's turn, she shied away from him, clinging to Miss IdaLee.

Maisie wasn't afraid of him anymore. Callie

had made sure Maisie was clear about that. But she was angry with him. And he didn't know what to do to change her mind. He didn't know what to do to convince her to forgive him.

Why should she? His conscience niggled at him. He hadn't forgiven Maisie's mother. Like father, like daughter?

Miss IdaLee, stronger than she looked, hefted Maisie into the wagon and into the arms of one of the waiting moms.

The old lady's violet-blue eyes softened. "I so admire a man who doesn't give up easily." She took his hand, her skin parchment-thin in his grasp as he handed her into the wagon. "Don't quit trying." Her gaze flitted toward the Apple House. "With either of our girls."

Was she talking about— His mouth dropped. She couldn't possibly mean—

He climbed onto the tractor. The matchmakers were nothing if not tenacious. Delusional, too, if they imagined a fine woman like Callie Jackson would ever consider a nobody like him.

She'd made herself quite clear on the terms of their arrangement. Even by Thanksgiving, he'd be fortunate to work up to "friends" when it came to the arm's-length redhead.

His parents. Tiffany. Now Maisie. He didn't understand why, but people found something inside Jake unlovable.

Jake headed into the orchard grove. No need

to give the usual farm talk with IdaLee along for the ride. Going into teacher mode, she expounded on the life cycle of Buzzy the Honeybee.

"May-zee a bee," his daughter piped.

His lips quirked.

"Maisie is a McAbee, not a honeybee," Ida-Lee corrected, but he could hear the smile in her voice.

In the Jackson household, Maisie was definitely queen bee. And everyone, including her, knew it.

Steering between the rows, Jake enjoyed listening to the curious questions the two-year-olds lobbed at Miss IdaLee. Questions she volleyed with ease.

Jake was more than a little proud his own daughter appeared to be one of the brightest of Miss IdaLee's students.

"Honeybees are our friends," Miss IdaLee continued. "They help our food, including apples, to grow. But their cousins the yellow jackets…"

Jake veered around the meadow.

"They look a lot like Buzzy the Honeybee, but if you bother them they can sting you many, many times. Some people get sick from the poison in their stingers. The yellow jackets are not our friends."

Gripping the wheel, Jake seconded that. Not his friends, for sure.

Returning to the Apple House parking lot an

hour later, Jake helped the children and their mothers disembark. When it was Maisie's turn he backed away, unsure what he should do.

Mrs. Fielding, owner of a nearby dude ranch, came to his rescue. Sizing up the situation, she lifted Maisie off the wagon and plunked her on her feet, thus averting another scene. She gave him a sympathetic pat as she headed off with her grandson in tow.

Jake blew out a breath. By now everyone in Truelove knew what a terrible father he was, how his own daughter couldn't stand him.

Putting distance between himself and this latest reminder of his innate inadequacy, he went to check the air pressure on one of the tractor tires. In deep conversation, Callie and Miss IdaLee lingered near the back of the wagon.

IdaLee appeared to be doing all the talking and Callie the listening. His cheeks burned when Callie flicked a guilty look his way. Was IdaLee talking about him? About them? He wished there were even a remote possibility there could be a *them*.

Whoa. He stopped short. Where had that come from?

Rounding the tractor, he came face-to-face with Maisie. She was just standing there, contemplating the big-wheeled tractor, unrequited yearning on her sweet little face.

Jake moved slowly, as if approaching a ready-to-bolt forest creature. Making sure she saw him coming. Giving her ample time to run if she chose.

She didn't. Run away, that is.

"Maisie…" It felt so good to say her name and not have her freak out.

His daughter's eyes darted to him, then to the tractor.

"Maisie…" He swallowed. "Do you want to ride the tractor?"

Her forehead puckered. She looked at Jake and then at the tractor once more, torn between tractor love and her determination to stay as far away from him as she could get.

Jake's heart sped up. Would she trust him? Would she come to him?

He opened his arms. "Maisie, do you want to ride the tractor with me?"

It seemed to him that, for a second, time stood still. That, for a moment, the birds fell silent. Miss IdaLee and Callie stopped talking. Like him, they were holding their breath and waiting for Maisie's next words.

Maisie's lower lip quivered, but she shook her blond tangle of curls. "Pop-Pop."

So Jake let her go. What else could he do? Arms outstretched, she ran to Callie.

A boulder weighed on his chest. Callie, not

he, lifted Maisie. Frustration and pain caused his eyes to well.

Would it always be this way?

His shoulders hunched, he climbed aboard the tractor alone and drove toward the barn.

Chapter Seven

Last week after the field trip, Miss IdaLee had made a few wise observations about the situation between Jake and Maisie. Upon reflection, Callie had come to believe that she was right.

Because of his past, Jake would never push forward where he wasn't wanted. He just wasn't wired that way. And if Callie waited for Maisie to make the first move, they'd be waiting forever.

Clutching the camera strap slung around her neck, Callie led Jake down the church corridor toward Maisie's preschool classroom. Brightly colored art projects—variations on a theme of autumn—adorned the walls.

She would need to be proactive in putting Jake and his daughter together at every opportunity. He had become such a big part of the orchard—like he'd lived here his entire life. Like he belonged.

Her heart clamored. What felt like a hundred

monarch butterflies fluttered in her chest. That was exactly what just the thought of Jake McAbee did to her, and even more when he got within ten feet of her.

She cut her eyes at him, striding alongside her with his hands stuffed in his pockets. He was focused on the doorway at the end of the hall. Under the brown canvas jacket, his broad shoulders hunched. Preparing to do battle once more in a war to win his child's affections.

Lately, she'd caught herself wondering how his dark blond hair—slowly growing out—would feel in her fingers. Bristly? Or silky like Maisie's?

Her heart thundered. What was wrong with her? She ran her hand down the side of her jeans. If only the yearning were as easily erased.

Over the past six weeks, she'd spent a lot of restless nights thinking about him. About him and Maisie. About the way he made her feel.

Jake came to an abrupt halt at one particular picture on the blue-painted wall. He pointed at the clouds of green on thin brown stilts and the blobs of red. "Maisie?"

She looked closer and nodded. "Maisie's rendition of the orchard." Then she frowned.

Among a cluster of red-dotted trees, Maisie had drawn three stick figures. A man, a woman and a little girl. Callie's heart sank. Jake didn't need her to tell him he wasn't included in Maisie's depiction of home.

His gaze dulled. "Maybe it's better if you attend Parents Day without me."

She caught hold of his sleeve. "But you wanted to see her schoolroom. Meet her friends."

He stared down the empty hallway. "I wanted…" He sucked in a quick breath. "I just wanted a picture in my head to take with me."

Already mid-October, the weeks were rushing by. In little more than a month—per their agreement—he'd leave for good. As would any hope that he could ever be more than Maisie's long-distance dad.

Wasn't that what she'd wanted? Her stomach twisted. The thought of saying goodbye—of never seeing him again—brought only a sense of impending doom.

Now, after a lifetime of rejection, he looked ready to bolt.

She tugged on his sleeve. "We have to keep trying, Jake. Please." And no longer able to deny herself, she took hold of his hand.

Jake's gaze fell to her fingers twined in his. "Callie?"

Heat suffused her cheeks, but she didn't let go of him.

Frankly—and this was part of what kept her awake at night—she was beginning to wonder if she ever could.

His work-hardened, calloused palm fit like a glove around her hand. Strong and warm against her skin, his hand felt right in hers. Right where she belonged.

Callie's pulse leaped. This wasn't supposed to be happening. Not with Maisie's father. Not with the man Tiff had betrayed.

She took a deep breath. She needed to get herself together. No matter what he did to her nerve endings, this was about Maisie. She had to keep this about Maisie. "Parents Day, Jake."

A quizzical look in his eyes, he searched her face for a second before squeezing her fingers. "Maisie." He exhaled.

Callie pulled him into the classroom, but he hung back behind her. At several pint-size tables, children worked on a pumpkin craft with their dads. He scanned the room looking for a certain small blonde with a head full of curls.

Maisie listened with rapt attention as Deirdre Fielding read from a book about Johnny Appleseed.

"See how they're sitting?" Callie motioned to the children on the big green rug. "Criss-cross applesauce."

Jake's mouth curved. "What else?" He leaned so close his breath brushed a tendril of hair at her earlobe.

She fought a shiver at the sensation on her skin. She tried not to be too obvious as she breathed in the masculine, woodsy scent of him.

At the refreshment table, several moms called

out their greetings. Miss IdaLee came forward with a welcoming smile. "So glad you both could join us."

But when Maisie spotted her father, she went stiff as a board.

"Stubborn as a mule," Callie murmured under her breath.

With her defiant little chin raised, Maisie stood up. Jake let go of Callie's hand, to her regret. Catching hold of the hem of Callie's black sweater, Maisie firmly pulled her to the other side of the small classroom. Basically, as far from Jake as she could manage.

From the dress-up box, Callie watched him survey the room—the shelves of picture books, the little tables and chairs, the paint easel. Memorizing everything he could about the life he'd never get to live with his daughter.

That awful realization and the guilt that accompanied it momentarily robbed Callie of breath.

Eyes blurring, she helped Maisie step into a princess costume. Fumbling to raise the bodice to her chest, Maisie scowled as Jake approached. "No Daddy, Cawee," she grunted.

He scraped his hand over his face. "I think it would be better if I wait for you over at the café."

"Jake—"

He held up his hand. "Stay. Enjoy the party."

"But—"

"Staying in Truelove, I'm being selfish." He scrubbed his neck with his hand. "The last thing in the world I want to do is make her unhappy."

Fear lanced her heart. Was he thinking about quitting? Leaving Maisie...them?

"Jake..."

He shook his head. "It's okay."

But it wasn't, not by a long shot.

"You'll w-wait for us?" She couldn't control the quaver in her voice.

His blue eyes darkened. There was more to what she was asking about than today, and they both knew it.

"I'll wait for you."

"Cawee..." Maisie tugged Callie into a crouch.

Tilting his head, Jake gave her a crooked smile. "She ought to call you mommy, don't you think?"

Callie sat on her heels. "But I'm not..." She bit her lip. "Tiff is her mother." Her gaze cut to Maisie, but losing interest, the little girl had wandered over to select a tiara.

"Tiffany is dead, Callie. You're the only mommy Maisie will ever have." His eyelids drooped. "Soon she'll start wondering why everyone else has a mommy. Start wondering if something is wrong with her."

Had that once happened to Jake?

A hole opened in her heart. She longed to reach out to him. To touch him. To comfort him.

But she dared not in this room full of parents and their children. In front of a Truelove matchmaker. Besides, she didn't have the right.

Not with the secret she was keeping.

She moistened her lips. "Maisie will have a Callie."

"Take it from someone who knows." His chin dropped. "A Callie is pretty great, but a mommy is the best."

"Maybe when she's older. When it feels natural—"

"I trust your judgment, Callie, to always do what's best for Maisie."

His words pricked her heart, sparking guilt for not trusting him with the most fundamental of issues. But before she could frame a reply, Maisie took Callie's face between her small palms.

"Look me, Cawee."

By the time she wrenched free and turned toward the door, Jake had gone.

Bells jangled as Jake pushed into the crowded diner. The buzz of conversation died for a moment as every head turned in his direction. *The flatlander.* That was what locals called people "not from around here."

After spotting an empty booth along the outside wall, he eased onto the cracked red vinyl seat. Conversations resumed as the people of Truelove went back to their business. Judging from what he'd observed, minding their own business was not something anyone in Truelove was accustomed to.

Welcome to Small Town, USA.

He pulled the plastic-covered menu from between the salt and pepper shakers, then laid it on the slightly sticky Formica tabletop. Aromas of bacon and eggs permeated the cheery café. On trips to the hardware store with Nash, he'd passed The Mason Jar many times. But the orchard had kept him too busy to stop by until now.

A favorite town hangout, according to Callie. An unofficial community center. GeorgeAnne and ErmaJean hunkered at a table in front of a large wall-mounted bulletin board. He grimaced. The Mason Jar—operation central on the busybody grapevine.

Miss ErmaJean fluttered her plump hand at him. Miss GeorgeAnne raised her eyebrow. No doubt she was wondering why he was a no-show for Parents Day.

She needn't worry. Her sources were far-flung and accurate. Within the hour, he felt sure she'd learn the entire sorry debacle of his first visit to Maisie's preschool. Especially since their missing third compadre was Miss IdaLee herself.

They meant well. He'd learned that much about them. They were genuinely rooting for him and Maisie.

Which he appreciated. Almost as much as the

sense of sanctuary he felt in the little chapel. Attending services with the Jacksons, the longing within him to know more only grew stronger with every passing Sunday.

And thanks to a few conversations with Nash, Jake was learning more about what made the Jacksons and the folks at the chapel so different from anyone he'd ever known.

There was a flurry of activity in the diner this morning. A waitress bustled around, refilling coffee cups. Through the swinging door, another waitress hustled out of the kitchen, a platter of steaming-hot pancakes balanced on her shoulder.

At the cash register, in the same casual jeans as the other waitresses, Amber Fleming gave him a distracted wave as she rang up a patron's bill, letting him know she'd be right with him to take his order. Callie had introduced them at church.

Behind the long white counter and cherry-red stools, the short-order cook passed plates through the cutout window for pickup. Tables and chairs lay scattered throughout. Through the plate-glass windows, booths overlooked Truelove. The town square. The post office. GeorgeAnne's family hardware store. The library. The bank.

Nothing much to write home about—if he had a home or anyone to write to. But strangely, Truelove was enough. Satisfying something deep within himself he'd never known was there until now.

Amber stopped at his table, removing the pencil she'd tucked behind her ear. "What can I get you?" Her long-sleeved navy T-shirt bore the words, Bless Your Heart, superimposed over the outline of a Mason jar.

He didn't feel like eating, not after what had happened with Maisie at Parents Day. But he was occupying a booth and he supposed he ought to order something. "Coffee."

She stopped writing, pencil poised over the pad. "That's all?"

He nodded.

She tapped the eraser against her cheek. "Cream?" She nudged her chin toward the sugar packets beside the ketchup bottle. "Sweetener's on the table."

"No, thanks."

She pushed off, her blond ponytail swinging. "Black it is, then."

Amber returned with two porcelain mugs. Setting one white cup in front of him, she slid into the other side of the booth across from him.

"Thought we ought to get better acquainted, seeing as how you're Maisie's father." Her sky blue eyes regarded him with an unexpected shrewdness. "And since you've become such a special part of my best friend's life."

Mountain girls weren't shy about speaking their minds. And they were fierce about protecting those they loved.

He squared his shoulders. So was he.

"Your twins spend a lot of time with Maisie."

She shrugged. "Because Callie and I spend so much time together. When time allows, of course, considering my night classes, Callie's photography projects—"

"Order up!"

At the summons from the cook, Amber jumped out of the booth.

He frowned. "What photography projects?"

Amber edged away. "Be right back."

Callie had taken her camera when they went to the preschool earlier, but the Nikon was so much a part of her, he barely took note of it anymore.

That was Callie—always snapping pictures of Maisie, filling a new album. Documenting his daughter's every developmental milestone. Perhaps she'd give him a few photos of the autumn he spent with his child that he could take with him when he left.

Yet, while he had a few minutes alone with Amber, he had more pressing concerns. Questions maybe only she could answer.

He sipped his coffee until she dropped back into the booth.

"Finally, the breakfast rush is over."

He took a quick look around. The crowd had thinned, including the matchmakers, who'd vacated the premises.

Great. Already it felt easier to breathe. He truly

appreciated their support for him and Maisie, but the ladies had proved embarrassingly insistent on pushing him and Callie together at every opportunity. Being paired with him must mortify Callie.

"So it's just you and your girls?"

Amber pressed her lips together. "No Mr. Amber in the picture." She snorted. "Nor likely to be."

"That's not what I meant. Callie mentioned..." He lifted the mug to his lips.

Blue fire flashed in Amber's eyes. A pretty woman. Smaller boned than Callie. But not his type. He preferred red—

He choked.

Yanking a handful of napkins out of the canister on the table, she thrust them at him.

"Th-thanks," he sputtered, still coughing.

"Single mom. I was the talk of the town before—" She lowered her gaze, wrapping her hands around her coffee mug.

"Before Tiffany came back to town."

Amber looked at him. "Yes."

"That's what I wanted to ask you." He leaned forward. "Things I can't ask Callie."

Amber's shoulders relaxed a notch. "Can't ask because Callie's middle name shrieks loyalty. Even when a person—me, you, Tiffany, take your pick—doesn't deserve it."

"This is going to sound odd, since I was married to her," he said with a grimace. "Though only for about a minute. Callie said you grew up in Truelove, too." He continued in a rush of words, afraid if he slowed down he'd lose his nerve. "You must have known Tiffany. Were the three of you best friends? Would you tell me what you remember about Maisie's mother?"

Amber met his gaze head-on. "If you're asking me if I can explain why Tiffany did the things she did, I don't think anyone could, even Callie or Beverly Jackson."

"Beverly? Callie's mom?"

Amber nodded. "The three of us played together when we were children. I don't know if you realized that Callie's mom was also a county social worker."

That explained so much about the person Callie had become. "Callie is a woman with a heart too big for her own good."

"Apples never fall far from trees, Jake. A cliché, but true."

His lips quirked. "And I've got the calluses to prove it."

For the first time, Amber gave him a genuine smile. "If you only knew how hard-to-impress Nash Jackson sings your praises."

There were only two people besides Nash

whose opinion of Jake mattered to him. Maisie. And Callie.

"Not only him." Amber tucked her tongue inside her cheek. "Miss GeorgeAnne. Miss Erma-Jean. And Miss IdaLee, too."

He rolled his eyes. "Save me."

She laughed. "Save us all once they get their hooks into you." Her smile faded. "They've given me up as a lost cause, of course."

He stirred. "Amber..."

She shook her head, stray tendrils of pale blond hair coming loose from her ponytail. She gazed out the window overlooking Main. "Looks like a happy place, doesn't it, from the outside looking in?"

"I couldn't have picked a better place for Maisie to grow up."

"And you'd be right. Truelove is a wonderful place. But nowhere is perfect. Only as perfect as the people who live there."

He nodded.

She ran the tip of her finger around the rim of the mug. "There are drugs and the crime they bring everywhere. Even here. Dysfunctional families." She cocked her head. "Despite how my life has turned out, I didn't come from one of those. But Tiffany did."

"I know about her father's abuse and neglect." He let out a sigh. "That was something Tiffany and I shared. Less-than-ideal childhood circumstances."

Amber's gaze sharpened. "But you rose above your situation. A poor start doesn't have to guarantee a bad finish. You've accomplished so much with your life. Your service to your country—"

He grunted. "The broken marriage… I still don't understand where I went wrong. And now I'm totally estranged from a child I love more than life."

Reaching across the table, she grasped his coat sleeve. "Don't assume everything is your fault. Tiffany came packaged with enormous problems. From what I've learned in nursing school, I think her mother was probably bipolar."

"Tiffany," he sighed. "She had some mental issues, too."

She patted his arm. "Beverly Jackson went above and beyond trying to help Tiffany break free of a destructive cycle. You did."

And if what Nash said was true about God, he had only by God's grace.

"I began to distance myself from Tiffany when the three of us got to high school. If there was trouble to be had, Tiffany would find it." Amber's mouth hardened. "She fell in with a bad crowd. Alcohol. Drugs. Ultimately, she ran away with one of the older boys. He was kind of an obsession for her."

His grip tightened around the coffee cup.

Amber slumped. "I shouldn't have said that to you."

"It's okay. It helps me understand what was going on inside her head. I'd rather know the truth." Jake took a gulp of now-cold coffee. "Lies are the one thing I can't forgive."

"Agreed."

From what little Callie had told him of Amber's past, Jake figured she spoke from bitter personal experience.

"I'm trying to put together in my mind a timeline for how things went down with Tiffany. What went wrong with us and when."

"All I know is that she ran away to Atlanta just before we graduated. We lost touch. Callie went to college. And I—" Amber's mouth turned down. "I'd say I made the worst mistake of my life, but then I wouldn't have my precious girls."

"I feel the same about Maisie. No matter what happened with Tiffany. Or what happens after..."

After November.

He'd made a promise, but it was getting harder and harder every day to imagine his life without Maisie. Away from the orchard. Apart from Callie.

Amber's lips pursed. "Out of the blue, Tiffany shows up at the orchard pregnant. The rest you know. I'm sorry I can't tell you more."

Still no explanation for why Tiffany walked out on him while he was deployed. Maybe he'd never find an answer. Or perhaps he'd known all along. Usually, the simplest explanation was the right one. Tiffany had used him to get his combat pay.

From what Amber had said, it was probably to buy drugs. Tiffany had never loved him. And when she found herself saddled with an unwanted baby—his baby—she'd run again.

A pattern with Tiffany. He was so thankful, though, that when she ran she hadn't ditched Maisie somewhere unsafe. For that, he'd always be grateful to Tiffany.

"What you've told me does help, Amber. More than you know."

She examined the clock on the wall. "I better get to work." She extracted herself from the booth. "But I am glad you're a part of Maisie's and Callie's lives."

With Maisie, not too much longer, though. As for Callie?

A hope he dared not dream.

Chapter Eight

The next afternoon found Jake working at the top of a ladder in the orchard. Plucking an apple off the limb, out of the corner of his eye, he watched Maisie playing below.

Not a preschool day, so Callie was helping them out. And on the trips back and forth from the grove to the cooler, Maisie got to ride the tractor with Callie to her heart's content. Full of her usual energy, Maisie ran over to where Nash worked at the other end of the long row.

"Bin's full. I'm taking this load," Callie called to him. "You okay?"

"Fine. Go ahead."

"I'll be back soon." Callie glanced around. "Maisie's with Dad."

"Okay."

Climbing aboard the tractor, Callie cranked the engine. After lifting the wooden pallet on the tines of the forklift, she headed down the grassy lane toward the outbuilding near the store.

Maisie ran toward the tractor, disappearing over the rise. "Cawee! No weave me!"

Nash had likewise disappeared. Probably on another row, out of sight somewhere within the canopy of gnarled apple branches.

"I'm still here," Jake called down. "Soon as she gets the apples refrigerated, Callie will be back."

Her set mouth told him Maisie believed him a poor substitute for her beloved Cawee. He'd agree with her on that.

Jake kept an eye on her as he continued to pick the apples. She found an old stick and began to run in circles around the tree.

He leaned against the ladder. "Don't run with the stick, Maisie. You could hurt yourself."

She stopped running, but she narrowed her eyes at him. He sighed.

From his high vantage point, he gazed over the orchard. He could see Callie talking to one of the seasonal bakers outside the Apple House. If the store had run out of a certain variety, she might need to grade some apples before returning to the orchard.

So it was just him and Maisie, much to her displeasure as she banged the stick against a nearby tree. He felt as hopeless as he'd ever felt about his daughter. She was never going to trust him again. She hated him.

He cut his eyes at Maisie. She whacked at the high grass beyond the mowed path between the row of trees. Thinking of snakes, he descended a few rungs. "Maisie, you need to put the stick down and stay out of the grass."

She ignored him and thwacked the earth with even more force.

He came down a few more rungs, planting himself at ground level. "Maisie. Please don't do that."

From the stiff set of her shoulders, he knew she had heard him. She returned to the path, but she didn't drop the stick.

His heart turned over in his chest. He loved her so much, his beautiful child. After what had happened yesterday at her preschool, he was beginning to think the longer he stayed, the worse he was making things with Maisie.

She moved over to the next row. Peering between the trees, he kept her in his line of sight. Perhaps the best thing he could do for his daughter was to climb into his truck and get out of her life for good.

But he'd promised Nash to help with the harvest. The Jacksons needed him. It felt good to be needed by someone. To feel necessary, even if only for his strong back.

He caught the sound of an engine drawing

closer. Not the tractor. Callie drove the farm truck toward him.

Good. Reinforcements. His gaze darted to Maisie, jabbing the stick into the ground around one of the trees.

He removed the pick bag from his shoulder as Callie brought the truck to a standstill. She lowered the window.

Jake placed the bag gently underneath the tree and strolled over to the truck. "It can't be quitting time already?"

"Close enough." Callie's warm smile did much to thaw the part of his heart Maisie seemed determined to freeze out. "I need to run to the grocery to get a few things for the bakers, but I brought you something." She handed him a bottle of water.

"Thanks." He took a long swig.

"You'll be a professional apple picker before we're through with you."

He swiped the bottle against his forehead. "You and your dad are great teachers."

The cool condensation felt good against his skin. Though mid-October, at this altitude the sun blazed hot in the afternoon. But it was good work. Raised in the inner city, he'd never realized how satisfying it was to work outdoors. This was as close to perfection as he'd ever imagined he could get.

Callie's eyes held something besides admiration. Something too easy to misread. Not something he deserved from a fine lady like herself. Not for somebody like him.

Trouble was, he could get to like it here too much. Like her too much. He already did. On both counts.

"I have another one for Dad. Where's—"

Maisie gave a high-pitched shriek.

His gaze snapped toward where she'd been playing. She wasn't there. In just that split second of inattention, she'd wandered into the grass again.

An angry drone filled the air, overriding Maisie's screams. She must have poked a wasp's underground nest.

"Maisie!" Flinging open the door, Callie jumped out of the truck.

He threw down the water bottle. Grabbing a tarp from the truck bed, he raced toward Maisie.

"Run, Maisie!" Callie staggered forward. "Run to me."

Maisie had dropped the stick, but stood frozen as angry buzzing yellow jackets swarmed out of the hole.

"I'm coming, Maisie!" yelled Jake. "Daddy's coming!"

Callie ran behind him, but his longer legs ate up the ground faster.

"I'll get her, Callie," he cried. "Don't come any closer."

Sobbing, her chest heaving, Maisie's eyes were wide and round. She put her hands over her head in a vain attempt to keep the yellow jackets away from her face.

He reached her in less than ten seconds, but it felt like a millennium. In one fell swoop, he wrapped the tarp around Maisie. Swinging her into his arms, he took off toward the safety of the truck.

"Get in the cab," he shouted to Callie.

He winced as the swarm of enraged hornets attacked his back, his neck and his face. But they couldn't reach Maisie, enfolded within the tarp in his arms. She was still screaming, whether from fear of the wasps or because of him, he couldn't be sure.

Callie had the passenger door open and the engine running when he shoved Maisie inside. Scrambling after her, he slammed the door behind him. Wailing, Maisie crawled across the seat and clung to Callie. Her arms nearly strangled Callie.

She gunned the motor and took off. "Are you okay, Jake?"

He killed a few wasps that had followed them into the truck. "Check Maisie when we get to the house." He smashed the last yellow jacket against the dashboard.

With a screech of brakes and spraying gravel, Callie pulled to a stop outside the farmhouse.

Yanking Maisie out of the truck, she ran for the screen porch. The world out of focus, Jake lurched after them.

He fell up the steps and into the porch, letting the door crack against the frame behind him like a shotgun blast. Sitting in the middle of the concrete floor, Callie jerked off Maisie's T-shirt, checking her torso for stingers.

Jake felt like his head was on fire. Like it was about to explode. Swaying, he took hold of the wall for support. "Is she okay?" he whispered. His voice sounded tinny and faraway.

Callie stripped Maisie of her socks and shoes. "I think so. I've found one little bite, but—" She glanced at him. "Jake?"

He staggered, clutching his chest. She and Maisie went blurry. "I—I—I'm allergic," he choked.

"Jake!" Callie clambered upright, trying to reach him. "Jake, talk to me."

His throat suddenly tight, he couldn't answer. He couldn't breathe. And then, he couldn't catch himself. He was falling into darkness.

When his knees buckled, Callie caught Jake as he collapsed. His weight almost unbalanced both of them, but with her arm under his broad shoulders, she managed to lower him to the floor.

"Jake? Jake, talk to me. Jake, can you hear me?" Frantic, she felt for a pulse. His face was dotted with more inflamed red welts than she could count. And that didn't even take into account the stings underneath his shirt. He'd been protecting Maisie, keeping her safe.

Her father yanked open the screen door.

"Daddy! Jake—"

"I was too far to reach Maisie in time. Thank You, God, Jake—"

"He's allergic. He told me right before he…"

Nash stepped over Jake's prone form. Jake's face and lips were swelling by the second. Maisie had gone shockingly silent, curled beside Jake, her blue eyes wide and staring.

"If he is allergic, he probably carries an EpiPen somewhere in his belongings." Her dad knelt beside Jake. "The swelling is closing off his airway."

"He's dying, Daddy. We've got to do something." She had never been this afraid in her life.

"Go upstairs. Find the EpiPen." Her father's eyes darkened. "We've got seconds, Callie Girl."

She scrambled to her feet and took off for the kitchen. She pounded up the stairs, her breath coming in quick, short gasps. She threw open his bedroom door.

Where should she look first? If she guessed wrong, she'd waste precious seconds Jake didn't have to spare. If she made the wrong choice, Jake could die.

Please, God. Help me. Don't let Jake die.

Jerking open the drawers of his nightstand, she dumped the contents on top of the bedspread. Rooting around, she spotted the familiar yellow EpiPen 2-Pak box. She ran down the stairs.

Thank You, God.

But suppose she was already too late?

Callie bit off the low moan rising in the back of her throat and hurled herself through the kitchen and onto the porch. No one had moved.

Her father was hunkered over Jake's prostrate form. With suppressed sobs, Maisie's chest rose and fell rapidly. Even to Callie's untrained eye, she could see Jake's breathing had diminished in her short absence. Had she gotten here in time?

She waved the yellow box. "Dad!"

Her father's gaze snapped to hers. "We don't have much time."

After ripping into the package, she fell to the floor beside Jake. She snapped off the orange cap and plunged the auto-injector into his thigh. Flinching from the pain of the needle, Jake groaned.

Was it enough?

Her father gulped. "I called 911, but as far out in the valley as we are…"

The EMTs probably wouldn't get here in time if the EpiPen didn't work.

"Wait five minutes." Her father squeezed her hand. "Then use the second one." He gave her a solemn look. "Even if we had more, I'd be afraid to give him another injection without medical supervision."

Tears ran down her cheeks. She swiped them away with the back of her hand. How had this beautiful autumn day dissolved so quickly into tragedy?

"We should raise his feet higher than his head." She sprang up, eager to do something, anything, while her father kept an eye on the clock.

Her father took Jake's pulse again. "His blood pressure has probably fallen already."

She grabbed a stack of cushions from the outdoor recliner and tucked them under Jake's legs. It hurt her to look at Jake with his eyes swollen shut.

"An antihistamine." She jumped up again, unable to sit by and do nothing while Jake was struggling for life.

"Good idea," her father encouraged.

She ran into the kitchen and ransacked the cabinet above the coffee maker for their medicine stash. Finding what she was looking for, she unscrewed the tablet and, with her father's help, placed the powder under Jake's misshapen tongue to dissolve faster.

"It's time again, Callie."

She administered the second dose of epinephrine. In the distance came the whirring of a siren.

"They're here." Rising up, her father's joints

creaked. "I'll bring them around." He dashed out the door.

"Don't you leave us, Jake." She stroked his arm. "I won't leave you. I promise. You're going to be all right." Her vision swam as tears misted her eyes.

"You better be all right," she whispered. "You have to be. Don't leave me."

The emergency room doors whooshed open as Callie's father, with Maisie and BooWoo in tow, rushed inside the hospital. Callie rose from the hard plastic chair.

"How is he, Callie?"

She shook her head. "I don't know. As soon as they wheeled him in, they took him beyond the doors. Lorena wouldn't let me go any farther."

Callie had ridden in the ambulance to the Truelove Medical Center. She'd held Jake's hand the entire way.

"I couldn't leave Maisie at the store." Callie's dad took a steadying breath. "They're jam-packed with customers."

Callie held out her arms to the little girl. Maisie was so quiet and pale.

She cupped Maisie's cheek, looking deep into her eyes. "Any signs of an allergic reaction, Dad? Do you think she's in shock?"

"I checked her over. I washed the two stinger

sites with soap and water. She'll be right as rain soon as she sees her daddy is fine. She's just scared."

Maisie burrowed into Callie.

Her eyes welled. "Maisie's daddy saved her. He knew he was severely allergic, yet he ran to her without hesitation."

Callie's father touched the top of Maisie's silken head. "Of course he did. It's what a good father does. Doesn't think of himself. Only his child. Anything to save his child."

"But Jake might..." Callie wasn't sure how much Maisie understood about the word, *die.* "He might not make it, Daddy."

Her father pulled her into a hug. "I don't think the good Lord is finished with what He wants to do for our Jake. Nor with us, either, Callie Girl. We need to keep our faith."

"And pray," she whispered.

Her dad nodded. "Always take the deepest concerns of your heart to your loving Father."

She hugged him back.

Her father smiled. "After all, what kind of father isn't eager to hear what his precious daughter has to say—"

"Anytime. Every time," she finished one of his favorite sayings for him.

Her dad released her as the ER doctor pushed into the waiting room. "Jake McAbee's family? Anybody belong with Jake McAbee?"

"We're here." She stepped forward. "He belongs to me... I mean..."

The doctor didn't notice her discomfiture. "I want to monitor him overnight to make sure there are no further adverse reactions."

Her father scrubbed his hand over his face in unaccustomed emotion.

Balancing Maisie on her hip, Callie sagged with relief. "He's going to be okay? He can come home tomorrow? I was so afraid..."

"He's a fighter." The fiftysomething doctor patted Maisie's jean-clad leg. "That's a pretty little girl you and your husband—"

Red-hot heat ballooned across her cheeks. "We... She... I'm..."

"You did everything right. Saved his life. Bought him the time he needed to get here." The doctor gave her a faint smile. "You have a beautiful family, ma'am. Jake McAbee is a blessed man."

Callie opened her mouth. And closed it.

Her father grinned. "As are we to have him in our lives."

That, at least, was the truth. As to the rest, she swallowed. That was not how it was with her and Jake. It wasn't how it could ever be between her and Jake. Not after Tiff... Not after the secret she was still keeping for Tiff.

At what point, though, did her feelings—and she wasn't ready to put a name to what she felt for Jake—begin to outweigh what she felt increasingly certain was a misplaced loyalty to Tiff?

"When can we see him?" she whispered.

The doctor made a sweeping gesture. "The nurses have him settled. He's groggy, but I'm sure he can't wait to see both of his pretty ladies."

She blushed, but it seemed more awkward to correct his misunderstanding than to just let it go.

"Here's my card if you or your husband have further questions. Please don't hesitate to call if you need anything."

She tucked the card in her jeans pocket as they followed the doctor down a maze of hospital corridors. Was Jake really okay?

Her heart caught in her throat at the sight of Jake against the white sheets. The swelling was gone. His features were normal again, but eyes closed, he looked so vulnerable in the hospital bed.

Usually, he was larger than life. Soldier tough. The gruff exterior and the high walls hid his loneliness from everyone.

Everyone but her. She saw right through to his heart. Jake McAbee was a good, trustworthy man. And he wasn't alone. For better or worse, Jake had them now.

"I don't want him to wake up alone." She

headed toward a chair. "He'll be disoriented when he awakes."

"Right you are." Her father rotated his neck, trying to get the kinks out. "Quite a scare he gave us. I could use some coffee. How about you?"

She shook her head. "I'm staying right here."

He smiled. "'Course you are. Didn't figure you'd want to be anyplace else." He held out his hand to Maisie. "Want to go with Pop-Pop to the cafeteria?"

Yellow curls flying, Maisie gave a fierce shake of her head.

Callie's father swung open the door. "Our little girl needs some Callie time. It's been a frightening and confusing afternoon for all of us."

Later, her dad managed to coax Maisie out of the room briefly for a soft-serve ice-cream cone. Through the bed rail, Callie was clutching Jake's hand when he opened his eyes.

"Callie?" he rasped.

"I'm here. I told you I wouldn't leave you."

"Maisie…" He struggled to keep his eyes open.

"She's fine, thanks to you. My hero."

His eyelids fluttered. "No hero…"

She pressed his hand. "You scared me so bad, Jake McAbee." Her voice trembled. "Don't you ever do that again to me, you hear?"

He gave her a sweet, sleepy smile. "Yes, ma'am." He turned on his side and fell asleep again. Sleep was good for him. The medicine was giving his body time to heal.

Eventually, her dad left her at the hospital, promising to return and take Maisie home soon. There were chores to attend to on the farm. Hunkered alongside Callie, Maisie pressed her face against the cold steel of the bed rail. Her small face pensive, she peered at the sleeping Jake like a prisoner in a jail cell.

Maisie was still too quiet for Callie's liking. She couldn't imagine how frightening the swarming wasps must have been to a two-year-old. Then seeing Jake unconscious on the floor. The loud noises of the arriving ambulance. The pungent, nose-wrinkling antiseptic smell of the hospital.

Callie was torn between watching over Jake and being there for Maisie when she went to bed tonight.

Somewhere across the hall, a monitor beeped, rousing Callie from her reverie. Glancing down, she realized that Jake was awake, his eyes fixed on Maisie.

"M-Maisie?" He moistened his lips. "Are you okay, sweetheart?" He reached through the bars for her.

But Maisie shrank away. Anguish flashed across his features. However, he quickly shuttered his face, clamping his emotions down into the place where he kept his feelings.

Suddenly, the need to comfort him, to soothe away the stark pain in his eyes, became overwhelming. She rested her hand on his head. His hair scraped pleasingly against her palm.

"It's going to be all right, Jake."

He didn't open his eyes. "It isn't."

"Don't give up. I know somehow everything will be okay."

"You can't know that."

She didn't. *But, please, God, somehow fix things between Jake and Maisie.* Because the prospect of Maisie losing her father, and Callie never seeing Jake again, was unacceptable.

Everything had to get better.

It just had to.

Chapter Nine

A week since the wasp attack, nothing had improved between Jake and his daughter. And every single day, Callie's heart broke a little more at the hurt in his eyes.

Maisie refused to acknowledge Jake's presence, much less smile or even talk to him. Continually shying away from something as simple as Jake handing her a sippy cup. It was excruciating to watch.

He'd recovered from the wasp stings. Healing from the sting of his child's rejection? Maybe never.

Tension practically vibrated between father and daughter. Jake decided Maisie needed a break from him. This morning he'd packed for a return trip to the base to finish some paperwork in Fayetteville.

Callie missed him already.

In the family room, she tucked a strand of hair behind her ear. "Tell your daddy bye-bye, Maisie."

Squatting on the heels of her brown leather Mary Janes, Maisie ran the green toy tractor in circles around BooWoo. "No."

Jake's blue eyes clouded. "Maybe it's better that I go. Neither of us can go on this way."

Maisie didn't look up, but she was listening.

Callie's heart twisted. Jake wasn't only talking about a few days. He was thinking about leaving for good, what she'd wanted from the beginning. Only now she wasn't sure she wanted him to go.

For Maisie's sake, of course.

If only she knew how to get through to Maisie. If only she could help him break through the barricades to Maisie's heart.

She sighed. "Daddy's leaving, Maisie."

No response.

He crouched beside his daughter on the rug. "Goodbye, Maisie." He cleared his throat. "Goodbye, BooWoo."

Maisie's lashes flickered, but she said nothing.

Slowly, he rose. "This is goodbye, then." He slung the strap of the duffel bag over his shoulder.

Callie followed him into the hall.

"I'll be back." He paused at the front door. "A day…" He shrugged. "No more than two."

Her throat constricted. His leave-taking felt

so final, and she experienced an irrational urge to throw her arms around him.

She was being ridiculous. He'd just told her he'd be back. But somehow, without her realizing it, Jake McAbee had become an integral part of Apple Valley Farm. Her life, too.

Callie clamped her lips together. Better get used to it. The clock was ticking. He'd be gone in another few weeks anyway, and she had a feeling once he left Apple Valley Farm she'd never see him again.

"It's a long drive." She touched his arm. "Take care of yourself."

His gaze flitted toward the living room. "Maisie won't miss me."

She sensed he wasn't in the mood for more platitudes about how Maisie would eventually come around. She ached to make things right between father and daughter, but she didn't know how to get Maisie to open up to him.

"I'll miss you, Jake."

He blinked, his gaze returning to hers.

She flushed. "I—I mean, the orchard won't be the same without you, Jake."

"That's sweet of you to say, Callie."

At the husky note in his voice, she looked at him. They watched each other for what seemed an impossibly long span of time.

Breaking eye contact, Jake ran his hand over

his head. Her fingers twitched with the remembered feel of his hair against her skin.

"I guess I should be on my way." But he didn't seem in any hurry.

She hung on the door. "Would you let us know you arrived safely? Maybe a text." She lifted her face.

"I'd rather call." His Adam's apple bobbed. "Will you answer?"

She tilted her head. "I'll answer."

The corners of his eyes crinkled, the lines fanning out. Whistling a tune, he strolled out to his truck. She felt a little like singing, too.

Midday, her dad came inside for lunch. Maisie hunkered in her booster seat, BooWoo clutched under her arm.

"How are my girls this fine October day?"

Callie watched Maisie push the food around on her plate with her finger. "Good." Better than good. She hid a smile, anticipating talking to Jake later.

"I sure miss having Jake here." Her father cocked his head. "I'm guessing I'm not the only one."

She could feel the red creeping up her neck. "Maisie, what's wrong with your lunch? You love grilled cheese sandwiches."

Maisie scowled. "No."

And here Callie had believed they had the perfect child who'd completely bypassed the terrible twos. They would not be left unscathed. Was it the twos that made Maisie so contrary with Jake?

"Maisie, if you don't eat your lunch you will not get a snack after nap time." She arched her eyebrow at her father. "And no sneaking her treats, Dad."

He patted Maisie's shoulder. "What's the matter, Daisy Maisie?"

Maisie hugged BooWoo to her chest. "No hungwy."

Since when? Maisie McAbee was a good eater. She racked her brain to remember what parenting books advised when a child suddenly refused to eat. Had Maisie decided to test Callie's authority?

"Now, don't get yourself all het up, Callie Girl. She ate a good breakfast this morning, didn't she?" Her father shrugged. "Maybe she's just not hungry." He patted his still-lean belly. "A lesson I'd do well to learn. Don't eat if you're not hungry."

"The books say not to make a battle of food…"

He rubbed his chin. "If she gets hungry enough, she'll eat."

Perhaps he was right. He'd raised a child—her—after all.

But Callie didn't want to reward defiance. "Maisie, you may not want to eat, but you will sit at the table with your family until we are finished."

Maisie didn't look up once during the entire meal. Soon her father returned to the orchard. While

Callie set the kitchen to rights, Maisie went back to her toys.

At the unnatural quiet, Callie headed around the counter. The rug was empty. Her pulse quickened. "Maisie?"

She found the little girl in the front room. Thumb stuck in her mouth, Maisie peered out the window, her face pressed against the glass. BooWoo dangled from her hand. Callie frowned.

The thumb hadn't been an issue for more than a year. What was with this sudden regression into infantile behavior? Maybe Maisie was tired.

"I think BooWoo needs a nap, Maisie."

Removing her cheek from the windowpane, without protest Maisie trudged upstairs, dragging the stuffed cat with her. Callie lifted Maisie into her crib.

Her head on the mattress, Maisie tucked BooWoo under her chin. "Big-gull bed," she whispered, and closed her eyes.

Oddly reassured, Callie smoothed a stray lock of hair out of Maisie's face. "One day soon, I promise, Maisie."

When harvest was over and life became quieter again. But a life without Jake. Her stomach knotted.

Edging out of the room, she closed the door softly behind her. He'd become far, far too important to her. Perhaps a few barricades around her own heart were in order.

She jolted when the landline rang. Jake? Forget barricades. Dashing downstairs, she snatched up the phone on the third ring.

Her heart pounded. "Hello?" Her stomach did that crazy somersault thing at the sound of his voice. "Jake…"

She sank into an armchair. "No, I'm not busy." Perfect timing with Maisie down for her nap. "So you got there all right?"

Feet up and over the armrest, she settled in to hear about his trip. They talked for thirty minutes. He wanted to know what her dad had been working on without him. What she'd been doing. She smiled at his declaration that a fast-food burger at a drive-through was a poor substitute for lunch at her table.

With the phone cradled between her head and shoulder, she told him about Maisie's lunch behavior.

"Nobody knows Maisie like you do, Callie."

Goose bumps rose on her arms at the sound of her name on his lips. She liked his voice. Deep and gravelly.

"You'll do whatever is right and best. I'm confident of that."

Guilt fretted at her conscience. She didn't always do what was right and best. Or, despite Tiff's protests, she'd have tracked down Jake McAbee as soon as Maisie had been born. As for what she feared and dreaded the most?

What benefit could come from planting doubts in his mind? But, oh, the harm. A hornet's nest best left alone. Better not only for Jake, but also for all of them. Maisie, most especially.

"So what have you been doing?" She injected a falsely bright note into her voice.

They talked a few minutes more before he had to go to an appointment on the base. But unable to shake a strange foreboding, she remained in the chair mulling over telling Jake her worst fear. The incident with the yellow jackets had more than proved Jake's devotion to his child. His unshakable love. Yet every time she contemplated what could happen if she shared her doubts about Tiff with Jake…

Upstairs, Maisie called for her. Callie wasn't sorry for the distraction. She brought Maisie to the living room to play with her barn animals. Preoccupied and restless with nervous energy, Callie decided to clean out the kitchen cabinets. And the kitchen drawers. And anything else she could think of to keep her hands busy.

Removing the roast from the Dutch oven, again she noted how quiet the house was today. A house with a two-year-old in residence should never be quiet. Quiet meant trouble.

"Maisie?" Wiping her hands on her apron, she ventured around the island. "Where are you, Maisie?"

At the sight of the open front door, her breath

hitched. Rushing forward, she found Maisie perched on the porch step outside, staring across the lawn.

"Maisie?" Callie hadn't realized Maisie could open the door by herself. "What are you doing out here, honey?" She planted her hands on her hips. "You scared Callie. I didn't know where you were."

Fixing her gaze on the horizon, Callie made a deliberate attempt to slow her heart, beating in triple time. The days were shorter now, and the sunset was beautiful this evening. Streaks of pink and lavender bathed the sky over the mountain.

With a shuddery sigh, Maisie rose and turned toward Callie, her arms tightly clutching BooWoo.

Callie held out her hand. "It's time for supper. Pop-Pop will be coming inside soon." Her heart hammered, relieved to find Maisie safe.

This wasn't like Maisie. She knew better than to come outside without Callie. Maisie appeared determined to break all her boundaries in one fell swoop today.

After supper she would have a long talk with the little girl about wandering off. Maisie refused to eat her supper.

"You love carrots, Maisie." Brow furrowed, Callie angled a look at her father.

Bewildered, he shook his head.

"We pulled those out of the garden ourselves,

Maisie." She picked up the child-size fork. "Do you want Callie to help you with the green beans?"

Maisie buried her face into BooWoo's soft suede body. "No want Cawee," she whimpered.

"Dad?" Callie's chin wobbled.

Getting out of his chair, he bent over Maisie. "Are you feeling poorly, little sweetheart?"

Her face still hidden, Maisie choked off a sob.

Callie scraped back her chair. Brushing aside the curls, she laid her hand on Maisie's forehead. "She doesn't feel warm."

"Summer flu has been going around. Amber's girls were hit with a virus last week, weren't they?"

Callie nodded. "Maisie, honey, would you at least drink the water in your sippy cup?" She cut her gaze at her father. "We can't let her get dehydrated."

Her dad held the spout to Maisie's lips. "Drink something for Pop-Pop, little sweetheart."

Maisie took the cup and swallowed a few sips. But a single tear, like a drop of dew, cascaded down her cheek.

Eyes widening, Callie's dad looked about as panicked as she felt.

She caught the tear on the tip of her finger. "What's wrong, Maisie? Does something hurt? Your head? Your throat? Your tummy?"

Maisie shook her head.

He headed toward the landline in its receiver on the side table. "I'm calling Lorena. She'll know what we should do."

"Come here, honey." Callie opened her hands. "Let me hold you."

Maisie lifted her arms, and Callie took her over to the sofa. Speaking into the phone, her dad responded to Lorena's questions.

He clicked off. "She says to monitor Maisie's temperature and push the liquids. Maisie could be coming down with something."

Callie hugged the little girl closer. "I'll check on her every few hours after she goes to bed. Maybe she'll fight off whatever this is and be better in the morning."

"God willing, and the creek don't rise."

Listless, Maisie went into her crib without a word.

For the first time in a year, Callie turned on the baby monitor. She and her dad went to bed soon after. Loving someone was exhausting.

She slept fitfully, waking at midnight and three in the morning. Each time when she checked, Maisie appeared fine, her breath steady, her little chest rising and falling, and BooWoo clasped in her arms.

Beyond weary, Callie awoke at six. Throwing off the bedcovers, she stretched her arms above her head. Then realizing she'd slept through her 5:00 a.m. check-in, she scrambled off the bed.

In bare feet, she padded across the upstairs hall. Behind her father's door, she heard the shower running. Yawning, she shouldered open Maisie's door. And came to an abrupt halt.

She pushed her bed hair out of her face, but nothing changed. There was a roaring in her ears.

Adrenaline kicking in, she whipped around, searching the corners of the room. A futile gesture, but it gave her the three seconds necessary for her mind to process what her eyes were telling her.

The crib was empty. Maisie was gone.

Oh, God, help me. Where is she?

Callie raced out to the hall. The shower was still running.

She was hungry so she went to the kitchen...

Callie was about to rush downstairs when she noticed Jake's bedroom door ajar. Some instinct made her pause. She pushed the door wide.

She sagged into the door frame, relief almost buckling her knees. The relief was followed by a sharp welling of tears.

Head on Jake's pillow, Maisie lay curled on top of the bedspread, fast asleep. Somehow she must have climbed out of the crib. Definitely time for a big-girl bed. Then she glimpsed what Maisie had tucked under her cheek. Not BooWoo.

Maisie had taken one of Jake's shirts out of the bureau. Callie's eyes went blurry. Not just any shirt. The now-laundered shirt Jake had worn when he'd saved Maisie from the yellow jackets.

She wasn't sick. Maisie was missing Jake.

When Callie crawled onto the bed, Maisie's eyes opened. Callie lay next to her, resting on the other pillow. Her nostrils flared at the unmistakable scent of Jake. Old Spice. Fresh air. And something that was just Jake. Indescribably pleasing and wonderful.

His daughter had found the place she could be closest to him.

"My daddy gone," Maisie whispered. The little hollow at the base of her throat quivered like the quick, sudden flutter of a hummingbird's wings.

"Daddy's coming back, honey."

"Me mean to my daddy. He gone." Maisie burst into heart-wrenching sobs.

Callie gathered the child in her arms. "Daddy's coming back." She blinked away her own tears. "Daddy would never—"

She mustn't say that, because one day very soon that was exactly what Maisie's daddy was going to do. Drive away for good, leaving Maisie where she belonged—with Callie on the farm.

That was the deal they'd made, the price for allowing him the chance to know his child, to make up for the years he'd missed. Stolen years. Years Tiff had stolen from Maisie, too.

And it made Callie sick that she'd been Tiff's

willing accomplice. More than willing. For her own selfish ends. Anything to keep Maisie here.

She stroked Maisie's hair, but Maisie refused to be comforted. Her little body shook with the tremors of her inconsolable grief.

Callie couldn't bear to think of how Jake would feel when he left. The forlorn expression in his eyes as he faced a future without his child. How alone—once more—he'd be.

With no one to comfort him.

But she couldn't think like that or she'd never be able to send him away without Maisie. She couldn't bear to live without Maisie at the orchard... Callie shut the thought down. Maisie was her life.

Though wasn't that supposed to be God?

She straightened. "Let's call Daddy."

Maisie shook with the hiccupping aftereffects of deep sorrow, but she let go of Callie. Getting off the bed, together they located Callie's cell plugged in to the charger in her bedroom across the hall.

"It's going to be all right." She speed-dialed Jake's number. "Daddy will be so happy to hear your voice, Maisie." She smiled.

The phone rang and rang. Where was Jake? Why didn't he pick up?

Jake McAbee would never abandon his daughter. Not willingly. Unless something had happened. An accident?

"Pick up, Jake. Pick up," she rasped.

But it kept ringing. And voice mail didn't kick in.

Jake's shirt clenched in her small hands, Maisie had shrunk into a pajama-clad ball on Callie's bed.

"We'll try him later. After breakfast."

Maisie broke into tears. And this time, Callie felt like joining her.

Chapter Ten

Army paperwork complete, Jake left the base for the last time. He'd enjoyed the camaraderie and the opportunity to be a part of something larger than himself. The army had been like a family—or as near to one as a kid with his background could envision until he met the Jacksons.

En route to Highway 401, he drove past the Airborne museum.

He hadn't hesitated to leave his career once he'd found out he had a daughter, but Maisie's continuing aloofness had him considering rejoining again. His former commanding officer had made it clear if ever Jake changed his mind there'd be a place for him. But even if he hadn't made the deal with Callie, he couldn't remain at the orchard, not with the way Maisie felt about him.

And because of the way he was beginning to feel about the Jacksons.

It scared him how much he craved Nash's approval. As for his feelings for Callie? They were complicated.

Tightening his grip on the wheel, his knuckles whitened.

He'd learned the hard way about needing people. Since Tiffany had left him, the only one he'd dared let into his heart had been Maisie. And that wasn't turning out so well.

Loving someone was not only an exercise in futility, but a disaster in the making. Reinforcing the lesson he'd learned as a boy—not only was he unlovable, but loving anyone was a dangerous mistake.

He needed to go. Maybe sooner than planned. Although he'd promised Nash…

Jake didn't have much to show for his life other than his military service. But one thing he'd managed to retain—his good name and his word.

Yet as soon as the harvest was over, he had a decision to make. He could rejoin the army or pursue the job in Houston. Either way, he needed to put some distance between himself and the farm. Before he was wrecked completely.

At the prospect of walking away from Maisie forever, his throat caught. He suspected he was already wrecked. And would be for a long time. Maybe for good.

She'd be better off without him. Hadn't his

own father told him as much? Over and over again. Hadn't Tiffany's betrayal proved it?

He'd been a fool to allow himself to dream. Yet from the moment Callie contacted him, he'd begun to imagine holidays, birthdays, summers with his child. He was an idiot.

Jake should've known better. He'd never belonged to anyone nor anyone truly to him, and he never would. Time to cut his losses and move on. Again.

Loosening his hold on the wheel, he took a deep, steadying breath. Passing a furniture warehouse, an idea suddenly came to him. One final thing he could do for Maisie. One thing he could leave her. One last expression of his love.

Before he talked himself out of it, he pulled the truck off the highway and into the parking lot. A middle-aged salesman showed him around the store, but Jake wasn't sure what he should choose. And then he stumbled upon just the right one. Immediately, he could envision Maisie in this big-girl bed.

"I'll take it."

The warehouse guys helped him load it into his truck. Jake covered the box springs, mattress, wooden headboard and footboard with a canvas tarp. Rain was forecast for the mountains.

In blue overalls, the older of the two workers closed the tailgate. "For your daughter, you say?"

Securing the last bungee cord to keep the bed from shifting, Jake nodded.

"You'll need something else, too." He pointed Jake toward the mall across the street.

Jake had never been much of a shopper. He preferred to shop as if on a mission—identify the target objective, get in and get out. Inside the department store, however, he became completely overwhelmed by the amount of merchandise for girls. But a nice saleslady took pity on a single dad who had no clue what he was doing and narrowed the choices for him.

Yet again, he somehow knew which one Maisie would love, the one Callie would choose. The bedding would complement not only Maisie's budding personality, but would also fit right into the cheery farm decor in the rest of the house.

Laden with shopping bags, he was pretty pleased with himself when he finally left the store. Until he remembered he had one more errand to complete before he headed for Truelove.

Callie's warm, laughing brown eyes rose in his mind. He exhaled. Fat chance someone like him had for true love, no matter how well-meaning the matchmakers.

Detouring to the post office near his old apartment, Jake closed out his account for the box he'd rented. He'd never used it, but Tiffany had wanted it. Cleaning it out, he found a clutch of uncollected mail. Standing in the white-tiled corridor, he eagerly sorted through the contents.

Junk mail. Disappointment plummeted like a stone in his stomach. Past-due notices in Tiffany's name. He grimaced.

He stalked out to his truck. What had he unconsciously hoped to find here? No long-lost letter explaining her desertion, nor why she'd kept his child's existence from him.

What a chump he still was. Her actions had proved Tiffany never wanted anything from him but his combat pay. And he'd never seen it coming. A sucker born every minute, that was him.

A sour taste in his mouth, he yanked open the truck door. He stuffed the unopened mail into the glove box. Out of sight, out of mind. If only his failures with Tiffany and their daughter were as easily remedied.

On the interstate heading west, he remembered he'd forgotten to turn on his cell this morning. With one hand on the wheel, he used the other to fish it out of his pocket and power it on. He hoped no one had been trying to reach him.

Leaving his former life behind, he hunched his shoulders. Perhaps every time she slept in the big-girl bed her dad had bought for her, she would remember him. Think of him with belated fondness.

Fondness wasn't much, but it was more than he'd ever had before. All he could ever hope to have from Maisie. And because she wouldn't accept his love, the bed was all he could ever give her.

He prayed she would like it, imagining a shy smile on her face. How her blue eyes would sparkle after he put together her new bed.

Or, his heart quailed, would she reject the gift just because it came from him?

The fears and doubts of a lifetime came roaring back.

God, please help her to like it. Soften her heart to me. But if she won't...

Jake swallowed, hard.

Please give me strength to bear it.

It was late afternoon when he drove under the crossbars of the Apple Valley Farm sign. Driving past the orchard trees on either side, he broke out into a sweat.

There'd been enough time between Fayetteville and Truelove to work himself into a fine frenzy. Anticipating—dreading—Maisie's reaction to his gift.

And as was his nature—based on experience—he expected the worst.

Dust swirling in the wake of the truck, he sighted the farmhouse high on the knoll overlooking the apple trees. Despite his worries, his heart lifted as it had that first day. He'd never get enough of this place.

The solid stone chimney and enduring foundation. The wraparound porch with its breathtaking views. The tin roof under which he'd often drifted into peaceful sleep to the pattering din of raindrops. The welcoming red-painted door. Home.

Rolling to a stop, he steeled himself and switched off the ignition. Thrusting open the door, he got out, his boots hitting the hard-packed gravel. He'd felt less nervous storming terrorist strongholds in Kandahar. He closed the door to silence the dinging.

Callie came out onto the porch. With the sun low on the mountain horizon, the rays caught the red of her hair, turning it into a beautiful flame.

It wasn't only the house that made his breath catch. How could he have missed her so much in just thirty-six hours? His pulsed ratcheted.

In jeans and a long-sleeved plum-colored cardigan, she stopped on the topmost step. A furrow lined the bridge between her brows. She wasn't smiling. In fact, she looked downright unhappy.

Had something happened while he was gone? Maisie—

"My daddy! My daddy!"

He froze midstep. From the direction of the barn came a blur of motion. Barreling toward him as fast as her two-year-old legs could churn, Maisie raced across the lawn.

Before he could react, she threw herself at

him, nearly unsettling him. Her arms wrapped around his legs. Her hands clasped behind his knees.

She buried her face in his jeans. "My daddy. My daddy. My daddy."

Jake almost touched the golden tangle of her curls, but wasn't sure he should. She'd never welcomed his embrace before, and now he didn't know what to do.

Nash followed Maisie from the barnyard, his pace more sedate. Jake's gaze cut to Callie, softly crying.

"I've been trying to reach you for hours, Jake."

His gut twisted. What had happened while he was gone? Everyone seemed the same. The orchard appeared the same. Only Maisie—he had no explanation for Maisie's behavior.

"I—I had it off for a while."

Nash joined Callie on the porch. He put his arm around his daughter. "Probably you two just missed connecting. And in the hills, sometimes service is spotty."

Jake's eyes flickered from Maisie to the Jacksons. "What's going on?" His voice sharpened. "Why is she— What's wrong with Maisie?"

Nash hugged Callie. "Nothing's wrong, son. Everything has come right."

Jake shook his head. "I don't know what you mean." His hands hung awkwardly.

At the small tug on his pants, he looked down into the blue of Maisie's upturned gaze.

On her tiptoes, she raised her arms up to him. "My daddy?"

His heart pounded. Hands flexing, he wanted so badly to take her in his arms, but—

"It's okay, Jake." Callie came closer. "Please pick her up. She wants her daddy. That's all she's wanted since you left."

Bending, he lifted Maisie. Twining her arms around his neck, she laid her head against the curve of his shoulder. Nestling, until her cheek rested against the exposed skin above the open collar of his button-down shirt. His arms tightened around her.

His heart nearly stopped for the explosion of sheer joy in having his child want him, need him. He blinked moisture from his eyes.

"I—I don't understand." He gulped past the boulder of emotion lodged in his throat.

Nash smiled. "Prayers answered."

"Maisie thought you'd gone forever." Callie's mouth trembled. "I think it was only then she opened the door of her heart to you. She's been inconsolable believing she'd never see you again."

His daughter clung to him like he was an anchor and she was drowning.

"My daddy no go," Maisie whispered against his shirt.

He kissed Maisie's head, his beard stubble scraping the silken threads of her hair. "Daddy won't ever leave you again if you don't want him to, baby."

"Oh, Jake…" Callie's eyes shone. "This was the breakthrough we've been hoping for. I told you she just needed time."

Thank You, God. Thank You for restoring the heart of my precious child to me. This is You. All You.

"I never really believed this day would come…"

Nash gave Jake a half smile. "When everything seems hopeless, that's when we must hold on to our faith. We're on that journey with you, Jake. All of us, no matter how long we've walked with our Father."

The journey of a lifetime. Jake would think on Nash's words later. Process everything in a quiet moment. But now—the gift.

"I hope neither of you will object." His chest heaved. "But I bought something for Maisie."

Maisie's little head popped up. "Me?"

"For you." Nash came around to the truck bed. "The one and only, Daisy Maisie." Lifting a corner of the tarp, he grinned.

Callie moved to see. "What is it, Dad?"

"It's a *b-i-g*…" Nash winked at Jake. "*G-i-r-l…b-e-d.*"

"Oh, Jake." Callie clasped her hands under her chin. "She's going to love it."

He shifted Maisie deeper into the crook of his arm. "Maybe you wanted to pick it out yourself."

Callie fingered one of Maisie's curls. "I think it is perfect that her daddy got it for her."

Maisie bounced. "Me see, my daddy. Me see."

"Not so fast." Callie laughed. "I think your daddy wants it to be a surprise, Maisie."

"Why don't you let Callie hold you while Pop-Pop and I—" Jake tried peeling Maisie off him.

She protested, her legs wrapped around his torso like a monkey on a branch.

He touched his forehead to hers. "Daddy's not going anywhere. But it's going to take both Pop-Pop and me to get your surprise ready."

Maisie placed her small palm against his cheek. "Pwomise?"

He thought his heart might burst from his chest. "I promise, baby."

"'Kay, my daddy."

When he set her on the ground, Callie took Maisie's hand. "Let's get supper ready and, afterward, your daddy can show you the surprise." She glanced up. "Or will you need more time to put it together?"

Nash clapped Jake across the shoulders. "I think between the two men who love Maisie the most, we've got it covered, daughter."

He and Nash carried the pieces of the bed upstairs.

As a weapons specialist, Jake could take apart

and put together every weapon in the arsenal, but facing the booklet of instructions, it was Nash who took the lead.

"Feeling a bit dazed is to be expected." Nash handed him a cordless screwdriver. "Maisie has staked her claim and now you, Jake McAbee, belong to her forever. As her heart belongs to you."

He'd never belonged to anyone before. Nor anyone to him. Tiffany's abandonment had only underscored that harsh reality.

"So why does this feel so scary and exhilarating all at the same time?" Crouching beside the metal frame, Jake rested his hands on his knees. "Is it always going to feel like this?"

"Yep." Nash unwound the protective packing material from the scalloped wooden headboard. "Better get used to it. Part of being a parent."

Brow creasing, Jake looked at him. "Part of being a parent involves sheer terror?"

"Sure does. Because now you know what it feels like to have your heart walking around outside your body." Nash leaned the headboard against the wall. "A raw vulnerability that comes with the urge to protect. But on the flip side, there's nothing like the sweetness of your child's smile."

Jake felt bewildered, slightly off-kilter, yet happier than he'd ever been in his life.

They'd finished—barely—when Callie called them to supper.

Nash repacked his toolbox. "I 'spect you better get Callie Girl to do the accessorizing."

Jake gathered the discarded packing material. "If we can keep Maisie downstairs after supper."

Nash broadened his chest. "A walk in the orchard with her Pop-Pop ought to keep her occupied."

Downstairs, Maisie launched herself at Jake again. She lifted her arms. "My daddy."

Huddled together in the kitchen, Nash filled Callie in on their plan. Maisie was too excited to eat, but when Callie insisted, Jake stepped into the fray, as well.

"Maisie, you need to do what Callie says."

Her little mouth pursed, but she picked up her fork. Across the table, Callie gave him a grateful look.

Later, while Nash and Maisie strolled through the trees in the twilight of evening, he headed upstairs with Callie to Maisie's bedroom. His heart started thumping erratically again.

Would she like what he'd bought Maisie?

Chapter Eleven

Maisie's eyes widened at the sight of her big-girl bed. Her little hands flew to her mouth.

"Does she like it?" Jake whispered to Callie.

Maisie danced on her tiptoes. "Oh. Oh. Oh."

"She likes it a lot." Callie held out her hand to Maisie. "Come see the big-girl bed your daddy bought you, Maisie."

BooWoo clutched under her arm, the little girl crawled onto the bed. The robin's-egg blue of the scalloped headboard and footboard was lovely.

Jake stuck his hands in his pockets. "Nash and I set the frame low. As she grows, it can be adjusted higher off the floor."

Propping BooWoo against the pillow, Maisie ran her palm over the colorful pastel squares of the bedspread.

Jake crouched beside the bed. "Your favorite colors." He glanced up at Callie. "I think."

Callie sat beside Maisie. "Pink, green, lavender and yellow *are* her favorite colors." She flipped back the comforter. "Look at your new sheets."

Maisie gave a tiny squeal of happiness and slid underneath the covers. Callie had never seen her so happy. The pink rosebud sheets were perfect.

"You did great, Jake McAbee. Really great."

He chewed his lip. "You think so?"

"You thought of everything." She gestured. "Fluffy shams and matching curtains, too. A little girl's dream bedroom."

"Just so it's Maisie's dream."

Maisie flopped backward and laughed.

Callie tilted her head. "I think it's Maisie's dream and more come true."

"As long as she's happy."

Callie smiled. "You've made your daughter so happy today. And not just because you bought her a big-girl bed."

Throwing off the covers, Maisie sprang forward and hurled herself at him. "My daddy, tank you, tank you, tank you."

He pressed his lips to the top of her head. "You're very welcome, my Maisie." He smiled at Callie. "Her hair smells like strawberries. And sunshine."

Maisie tugged her father onto the mattress next to Callie. Her arms went around them both. And Callie found herself physically closer to Jake than she'd ever been before. Her heart turned over.

Quickly, he freed himself from Maisie's tight embrace. The smile slid off his face, replaced with the aloofness she'd come to know all too well. A pinprick of tears stung her eyelids. Being close to her made him uncomfortable.

Hollowness bottoming in her stomach, Callie inserted a few more inches, keeping Maisie's warm, pajama-clad body between them.

Was he still hung up on his ex-wife? Or after what Tiff had done, would he never trust another woman again? Callie's relationship with the woman who'd hurt him most made her the last person on earth with whom he'd ever open up.

Her lower lip quivering, she got off the bed. "Bedtime, Maisie."

Maisie wound her arms around her father's neck. "No bed."

Callie folded the cardigan around her body. "Yes, bed."

Letting go of Jake, Maisie bounced, testing the mattress.

"No, ma'am." Callie took hold of her. "No more jumping on the bed, little monkey."

Maisie laughed. "May-zee no monkey." Leaning against her father's strong, muscled back, her eyes flitted to Jake. "Pway night-night with me and Cawee, my daddy?"

A lump rose in Callie's throat. Maisie had hardly let go of her father since he'd returned. As if she were afraid if she couldn't touch him, he'd vanish again. It wasn't just the big-girl bed she loved.

"She wants you to pray with her before she goes to sleep, Jake."

One arm supporting Maisie, he scrubbed his other hand over the stubble sandpapering his chin. "I don't know how to pray, Callie."

She ran her gaze over the angular line of his jaw, the craggy shape of his brow. To the uncertainty in his blue, blue eyes. "It's just talking to God. Right, Maisie?"

Maisie pulled at him.

"You don't have to say anything if you don't want to, Jake. She just wants to keep you close for as long as possible until she falls asleep."

"I can do that," he rasped.

His hand shook as he tucked Maisie—and BooWoo—into bed. Callie stationed herself at the footboard. He loved Maisie so much. How could Tiff have denied him this?

Callie clenched her fist about the rounded bed knob. How could she continue to keep Tiff's secret? But after everything Jake and Maisie had gone through to find each other, would telling the truth only make things worse? It wasn't like she knew one way or the other for sure. The real truth was that Jake needed Maisie, and Maisie needed him.

When Jake knelt beside the bed, Maisie smiled. "Me pway fuwst, my daddy, 'kay?"

He took her small hand in his large one. "You pray first, baby."

Closing her eyes, Maisie lifted her face to the ceiling. "Thank You, God for Cawee... For Pop-Pop... For BooWoo... For tractors..."

Looking over his shoulder at Callie, Jake rolled his eyes.

Farm girls, she mouthed.

His lips twitched.

"...For 'appy juice... For my big-gull bed... For my house..." Maisie laced her tiny fingers into Jake's. "And my daddy."

Bowing his head, Jake squeezed his eyes shut.

"My daddy pway now."

His Adam's apple bobbed. "Thank You, God, for my Maisie..."

Beneath the sheet, Maisie wiggled in happy delight at the sound of her name.

"For Maisie's Pop-Pop, for this home, for BooWoo..."

"For Cawee, too..."

Callie gripped the footboard.

"For Callie..." His voice dropped to a whisper. "Th-the best mother Maisie could ever have."

Her heart skipped a beat. And despite keeping Tiff's secret, she'd done everything in her power to give Maisie the best father the little girl could ever have.

Jake wasn't finished praying yet. "Thank You, God, for Callie, the best friend I've ever had."

She covered her mouth with her hand. Friends. What else had she expected him to say?

That was the deal she'd laid out with Jake from the beginning. Why now did she yearn for something more? Yet, how could she ever hope for more with Tiff's secret lying between them?

"And thank You, God, for...for..." He stumbled.

Was he thinking of Tiff? Suddenly, her chest ached with unshed tears.

"For tractors. Amen."

Maisie giggled as he probably meant her to. Leaning down, Jake kissed Maisie's cheek.

She hugged him tight. "I wuv you, my daddy."

Callie watched Jake's face transform.

"I love you, too, my Maisie." One final quick hug. "Sweet dreams, baby."

Maisie's brow puckered. "Mowow?"

He smoothed a blond curl off her forehead. "Daddy will see you tomorrow."

Smiling, she reached for Callie. His hand on the light switch, Jake waited at the door as she and Maisie hugged good-night.

In the hallway, Callie softly shut the door behind them. From downstairs came the sound of the television. Her father's usual Thursday night football game.

But she didn't feel like joining him. Nor going to bed, either. Restless, she didn't know what she wanted to do.

Halfway down the staircase, Jake sank onto the carpeted step. "Want to talk for a while? Unless you'd rather—"

"No." She moved toward him. "I'm wound too tight to go to sleep."

Wound tight didn't begin to describe what she felt when she was near Jake. *Wound tight* wasn't the half of it.

He made room for her to sit beside him.

For a long moment there was silence between them. They both stared at the bottom landing, where it opened into the living room below. Her heart thrummed painfully in her chest.

What did he want to talk about? They'd talked so freely on the phone yesterday. But so much had happened since then.

She moistened her lips. "The big-girl bed was perfect."

"I figured since I'd be long gone by Christmas, the bed would be an early gift to her from me." He raked his hand over his hair. "I also hoped if she loved the bed, maybe she wouldn't hate me so much."

He was still leaving? Her stomach churned. It was getting harder and harder to rationalize that she was acting in Maisie's best interests by keeping the little girl on the farm.

"Maisie loves you. She's always loved you. She was just afraid to let herself love you."

His eyes flicked to hers. "Like father, like daughter, huh?"

Callie wasn't sure he was just talking about Maisie. Was she hoping he wasn't only talking about Maisie?

Beside him on the stair, Callie smelled like apples and cinnamon. Jake rubbed the back of his neck, trying to get his wildly beating heart under control.

Sitting this close to her messed with his head. She was Maisie's mom in every way that counted. There could never be anything but friendship between them. To reach for more would be to invite heartache and risk damaging this fragile beginning with his daughter.

Tiffany was proof he wasn't capable of sustaining a relationship with a woman. Somehow he'd managed to ruin his marriage. If he hoped to successfully co-parent with Callie, he couldn't afford to destroy the tenuous truce they'd established.

Strict boundary lines would be essential. High fences crucial. Because, after today, suddenly he had such hopes for becoming a real part of his daughter's life.

"I've been thinking—wondering—about where Maisie and I go from here."

Callie's eyes widened.

He held up his hand. "About where all of us go from here."

She squared her shoulders as if bracing for a blow. "What are your thoughts?"

How could he begin to unravel the tangle of emotion he felt when he didn't even understand it himself?

Jake rested the back of his head against the wall. "God has given me a piece of Maisie's heart today." He looked away. "Something I in no way deserved."

"None of us deserve His grace, but He gives it anyway." She angled toward him, only inches separating them. "And I think Maisie's given you more than just a piece of her heart."

His lips curved. "You think so?"

For the first time it occurred to him that if he truly wanted to make a fresh, new beginning in his life, he needed to extend the same grace to Maisie's mother. In keeping his child from him, Tiffany had greatly wronged him. But if, on his behalf, God would do this incredible transformation in Maisie's heart, how could Jake do anything less for Tiffany?

Please tell her I forgive her, God.

The boulder he'd carried for almost three years lifted. And he felt able to breathe deeply—really breathe—for the first time since he'd received the divorce papers from Tiffany's attorney.

Forgiveness. Two months ago, nearly an unthinkable idea. He'd changed since coming to Apple Valley Farm. This place had changed him. Knowing the Jacksons had changed him. Most of all, God's love had changed him.

And now Maisie's love had changed him, because more than anything, he wanted to be the father she deserved. A father she could respect and be proud of. In the truest sense of the word, he wanted to be her dad.

But he needed to talk through a more immediate issue with Callie. She was expecting—counting on—him to leave in a few weeks. He prayed for the right words to convince her to allow him to be more of a permanent part of Maisie's life.

"I thought I'd call my buddy in Houston. Let him know I won't be taking the job." He focused on the stair below them. "I'd like to settle nearby. So Maisie and I..."

Callie rocked back.

He opened his palms. "Maisie would stay here at the orchard with you and Nash. She belongs with you. That isn't going to change, I promise you, Callie. You've got nothing to fear from me."

She exhaled in a slow trickle of breath.

"After what Tiffany's likely told you, you have no reason to trust me—"

"I do trust you, Jake. It's Tiffany I..." She dropped her head, denying him access to her eyes.

Callie Jackson's expressive brown eyes were a window into her soul.

"We could make a formal custody agreement." He gulped. "If you'd allow me to spend time with Maisie. At your discretion, of course."

Callie knotted her hands. "I'd never keep your daughter from you, Jake. Especially not now. No matter what, she will always be your daughter. Yours." Her mouth hardened. "And no one else's."

She sounded angry, yet the anger wasn't directed at him. If not him, though, who? Maybe Tiffany. He wasn't the only one Tiffany had placed in a difficult position.

Callie tucked a fiery tendril of hair behind her ear. "And you will be here, Jake, to watch her grow up. Like a father should."

"I won't be here, here."

She stiffened. "You said—"

"Apple season will be over soon. You won't need me on the farm anymore."

Her chin came up. "That's not true. We will need you."

Jake shook his head. "I think it would be better if I moved out."

"But—"

"I can rent a room or an apartment in True-love. Whatever it takes to stay close to Maisie— I'll bus tables at The Mason Jar if I have to. Dig ditches."

"There's no reason for you to leave the farm." Her mouth thinned. "Do you hate it here so much?"

Hate the orchard? Was she kidding? This already was closer to home than Jake had believed he'd ever come in this life.

Yet, due to the emotions he felt for Callie Jackson, a little distance wasn't only wise, but entirely necessary.

To not reveal the depth of feeling she inspired within him. He fought the urge to run his fingers through her tawny tresses. Battling the need to touch her mouth with his lips.

Jake couldn't go there with her. "I don't think it would be wise for us to overcomplicate an already complicated situation, Callie."

Her eyes blazed. "You think so, do you, Jake McAbee?"

Jake fidgeted, not liking the low purr in her voice. "It's the smart thing to do, considering."

"Considering what?" She sprang to her feet, towering over him for once. "You should be careful what you wish for. Because one day, you might get it."

He'd figured she'd be glad to see the back of him since he always made her uncomfortable. Not for the first time did he think that women spoke a different language, which showed how little he'd ever understood women.

Crossing his arms, he rose. In the narrow stairwell, one deep breath and his chest would brush against her arm. He uncrossed his arms, determined to keep his distance.

High walls… Tall fences…

"You are the most…" She jabbed his T-shirt with her finger.

At the touch of her hand, a lightning bolt of fire and ice sizzled his nerve endings.

Her finger punctuated her words. "The most infuriating—"

Before he could stop himself, he caught her hand, loosely encircling her wrist with his fingers.

She gasped, her eyelashes fluttering.

"Whereas you, Callie Jackson, are the most lovely woman I've ever had the pleasure of knowing."

And suddenly the space between them disappeared.

Cupping her elbow in his palm, his other hand pressed into the small of her back. She didn't move away. Maybe he no longer made her so uncomfortable. Perhaps she didn't dislike him after all.

Swaying into him, she lifted her face, and the ache to taste her mouth intensified. He pulled her close. His heart jackhammering in his chest, he bent his head. He tilted his chin. Her lips parted and—

"Cawee! Wursty, Cawee!"

They broke apart so fast he fell into the wall.

Hand to her throat, she scrambled up the stairs. "Maisie's thirsty." Callie edged past him, her sweater scraping against his arm.

Jake scrubbed his face as she disappeared into Maisie's room. If Maisie hadn't called out, what would have happened with Callie?

This…this…attraction? Whatever he felt for Callie was exactly why he needed to leave the farm. Before something else happened between them.

Before the desire to kiss Callie overcame what he knew to be right. He could never be right for someone like her. And if he continued on this foolish path, he'd only succeed in losing the one person who'd ever loved him—his daughter.

He slipped into his bedroom. If Maisie hadn't called out, would Callie have kissed him back? Or spurned him like Tiffany?

It turned out to be a long night of staring at the ceiling.

Because, despite everything, he couldn't stop pondering what it would've been like to feel Callie's lips against his own.

Chapter Twelve

The next day the bell jangled over the entrance as Callie stepped inside The Mason Jar. The smell of hash browns, ham and eggs permeated the crowded diner. Behind the counter, coffee percolated on the burner of the coffeemaker. She scanned the diner for Amber.

Maisie had gone with Pop-Pop and Jake to the hardware store. A not-to-be-missed event for a farm girl like Maisie McAbee. She'd insisted Jake carry her down the sidewalk.

There was something about a strong man holding a child in his arms... Was there anything sweeter?

Callie had decided to make the most of her free time by seeking out Amber. She desperately needed an objective viewpoint on the crazy tangle of emotions she felt for Maisie's dad. And when she told Amber about what had happened last night—

That was the thing. She couldn't decide if she was happy or sad about what had not happened on the stairs.

Door swinging behind her, Amber emerged from the kitchen. On her shoulder, she carefully balanced a tray laden with plates of French toast. Callie took a seat in a recently vacated booth, waiting for her friend to deliver the order to a customer.

Spotting Callie across the room, ErmaJean and IdaLee waved. GeorgeAnne sipped her coffee. Callie nodded, but lest they mistake her politeness for an invitation, she directed her attention to her BFF at the nearby table.

Her wheat-colored hair slicked away from her heart-shaped face into a tight ponytail, Amber appeared thinner than the last time they'd talked, the shadows under her dear friend's eyes more pronounced. Callie reconsidered laying the burden of her troubles upon Amber's already overloaded shoulders.

But before she could beat a hasty retreat, Amber carried her now-empty tray over toward Callie.

"Hey, girl." Amber's blue eyes sparkled. "Let me clear the table for you—"

"Don't worry about me." Callie started to slide out of the booth. "You're busy."

Amber blocked her escape. "I'm due a break

anyway. Busing the table will give me a good excuse to linger."

Setting the tray on the table, Amber began loading the dirty utensils and glasses. "Besides, it's good to see a friendly face." She dropped her gaze, scraping the leftover food onto one plate and stacking the rest.

"What do you—oh." Callie's eyes widened. At the far end of the counter, Amber's estranged father hunkered on a stool, nursing his coffee. "Why is he here?"

Amber's lips flattened. "Because he wants to make sure I don't forget my mistake."

Callie frowned. "Or maybe he's just checking to make sure you're okay."

"Like he cares."

Callie pursed her lips. "Your father is a proud man. It's hard for him to admit he was wrong. To say he's sorry."

Amber's eyebrows lowered. "But he wasn't wrong. Not about that no-good ex-husband of mine."

Callie leaned over the discarded pile of napkins. "You're exhausted, Amber. You can't keep working at The Mason Jar all day and then take classes every night."

Amber smoothed her hands down her jeans. "I'm fine." But she wouldn't meet Callie's probing gaze. "Like my dad said, I made my bed hard and now I'll have to lie on it."

"My dad and I, we want to help."

Amber shook her head. "I appreciate the offer, sweet friend, but your family is swamped this time of year with apple season. I couldn't ask you to take on two more little girls."

Callie lifted her chin. "I happen to love little girls."

Amber smiled, and the tired lines in her forehead eased for a moment. "My girls love you and Maisie. Maybe after apple season…" The lost, forlorn look returned as her eyes cut toward her stiff-necked father. "But it's up to me to make a better life for us. And no matter what, I'm determined to show my father I can."

Proving it to herself, too? But Callie didn't say that.

Amber slid into the booth opposite Callie. "My love life may be in shambles, but you, on the other hand?" She grinned. "I'd say your love life is on an upswing."

Callie sniffed. "I have no idea what you're talking about."

"Tell me another one." Amber nudged her head toward the diner wall. "What's with that, though?"

Callie peered over the graying heads of Truelove's matchmakers to the community bulletin board. Squinting, she took in the notice tacked onto the corkboard.

Below the words *Looking to Rent*, Jake's name and cell number.

She slumped. "Jake thinks it would be better if he moved out of the farmhouse."

"Better why?"

Taking a deep breath, she gave Amber the condensed version of the events of the past seventy-two hours.

Amber's eyes shone. "I'm so happy Jake and Maisie have connected." Her smile fell. "That's what you wanted. Or not? I'm confused."

Welcome to the club.

"He's not taking Maisie away from the orchard, is he?" Amber half rose. "If that's what he—"

"Jake isn't planning to take Maisie anywhere. He believes she belongs with me."

"So why the sad face?"

"I'm not—" Callie bit her lip.

Okay, she was feeling a bit blue at the prospect of not having Jake McAbee around the farm. Though "a bit" didn't even begin to describe the myriad conflicting emotions she felt when it came to the ex-soldier.

"Why do I get the feeling I'm missing something? Unless you and Jake..." Her mouth dropped. "Did you and Jake... Did Jake *kiss* you?"

"I wish..." Callie sucked in a breath. "No, I

don't wish…" Groaning, her head fell back onto the seat. "I don't know what I wish."

Amber laughed.

She stared at the popcorn ceiling. "But with Jake moving out, I guess I won't ever have the chance to find out what I wish."

"Girl, you've got it bad."

Callie straightened. "I do not have it bad. He's Maisie's father. We've only known each other a few months."

"Not true. You got to know each other through email before you ever met." Amber shrugged. "Trust me, after my disastrous experience, slow and steady is the best way for a relationship to develop. So what are you not telling me, Callie Rose Jackson?"

Callie fiddled with a sugar packet. "Last night we were both so happy after what happened with Maisie that he… I…" She took a deep breath. "We almost kissed."

Amber jerked her thumb at the board. "Hence, his panic-induced reaction." Her nose crinkled. "Men. So typical."

Callie planted her elbows on the sticky table-top. "Jake's not like that. He's wonderful. He's smart. He's hardworking. He loves Maisie so much…" Her eyes misted.

"Maybe things were moving too fast for him last night. Some guys—especially quiet ones like Jake

McAbee—like to turn things over in their mind before they take the next step in a relationship."

"I'm not sure he'll ever be ready for another relationship." Callie's chin dropped. "Not after Tiff."

Amber's features closed. "Is this about Jake's inability or yours to accept his past? If him once being with Tiffany is a nonstarter for you, then it's better he move out now and you put him out of your mind."

Callie was disconcerted by the uncustomary glint in her best friend's eyes. But she'd struck a nerve. This was Amber's worst fear—that no man would ever be able to get past the fact she'd been married, albeit so disastrously, to someone else.

She snagged Amber's hand. She held on when Amber might have pulled away. "You deserve to find love again, Amber Dawn Fleming. It will happen. I know it will, someday."

"Perhaps someday." But Amber looked away as if she didn't believe her.

"And it doesn't matter to me that he was once married to Tiff. It's—" Callie clamped her lips together.

How could she have a relationship with a man from whom she kept secrets?

"What's holding you back?"

"It's complicated."

Almost Jake's exact words to her.

She scrubbed her forehead. "He's determined to move out. And after apple season, we'll return to being polite strangers. I'll probably only see him when he picks up Maisie to spend time with her."

Amber got out of the booth. "I wouldn't worry too much about him moving out."

"Why not?"

Amber balanced the tray on her hip. "Take a look—that's why."

Scraping her chair across the café linoleum, Miss GeorgeAnne rose and untacked Jake's notice from the bulletin board. She stuffed it into her voluminous quilted tote.

Callie shook her head. "But he'll only put up another one. All over town, too, I expect."

"And they'll take them down, each and every one." Amber wagged her finger. "I hear they've already put out the word. Woe to anyone who so much as offers him couch space. No worries. Jake McAbee isn't going anywhere."

Callie unfolded from the booth.

Amber batted her eyes. "You know how relentless the matchmakers are when they get a notion in their heads."

Callie was almost afraid to ask. "And what idea is that?"

"That Jake McAbee has found his true home in Truelove, North Carolina." Without losing her grip on the tray, Amber gave her a gentle hip bump. "True love on an apple orchard with his sweet little daughter and a certain home-grown, budding photographer."

"I'm not a—"

"You are a photographer, and if these ladies have anything to say about it, the three of you will get the happily-ever-after you deserve."

"Happily-ever-after?"

"I hear that's possible." Amber shoved off toward the kitchen. "At least, for some people."

After that heartrending statement, Callie wanted to call her friend back. But how could she explain Amber was wrong about her?

She'd perpetuated Tiff's cover-up. It wasn't Amber or Jake who didn't deserve a happily-ever-after. It was Callie.

His shoulders tensed. Jake didn't understand how, but he knew somewhere behind him stood Callie.

Whether he could see her or not, he always knew when she entered the same space he occupied. With her, it was like he had some kind of internal radar.

And whenever she got within touching distance…

His heartbeat accelerated. His pulse thrummed. His stomach tightened.

Swallowing hard, he turned around. Yep.

There she stood, framed by the barn door, the sun backlighting her hair.

He made a determined effort to breathe. Hard to do when she was as close as he'd gotten to her in a week.

A busy week. A week after that night on the stairs. And so far, no leads had panned out enabling him to move into a place of his own.

He'd gone out of his way to avoid her. Grabbing breakfast on his way out the door every morning. Finding an excuse to eat lunch outside the house.

But yesterday he came to the unsettling realization she wasn't exactly seeking him out, either.

At the dinner table she kept her gaze pinned on everything and everyone but him. Other than taking care of Maisie and manning the Apple House, she never ventured into the orchard anymore, or at least not when he was there.

Somehow she'd worked out this elaborate scheme of making sure when she was with Maisie, he wasn't. Or vice versa. But never together with Maisie at the same time.

He was pretty sure Nash had noticed. Nash was sharp. He didn't miss much. But as far as Jake could tell, Maisie hadn't noticed.

Getting to know his daughter was amazing. Spending time with Maisie was a dream he'd never dared dream after that terrible first day.

His dreams were coming true. All, except one. But he had no right to dream dreams about Callie.

Keeping his head down, he trudged past Callie, rehanging the hoe on the wall rack next to the barn door. Unable to help himself, though, he cut his eyes to her and, yes, she was still standing there. Just standing there. Looking at him and not saying a word.

The not talking this week had bothered him more than he'd foreseen. He missed talking with her about her day, sharing funny anecdotes about Maisie. He missed Callie's laugh. He missed her smile. The way her eyes lit when he walked into a room—

He was an idiot. Callie Jackson's eyes didn't light up for him. The reason he'd kept his distance no longer seemed so important, although the apparent ease with which she'd reciprocated only underscored what he'd feared from the beginning—he was easy to walk away from. Easy to forget.

"Jake?"

Straightening the already straight hammer on the worktable, he kept his back to Callie. "Is everything okay with Maisie?"

"Maisie's fine. B-but I'm not."

He stiffened at the breathy, hesitant quality of her voice, though it was good, so good, to hear her voice again. Talking to him. No longer ignoring his existence.

Jake angled to face her. "Did you need something, Callie?"

She'd stepped out of the doorway and into the shadows. He didn't like not being able to see her face. He'd come to rely on her expressive features to reflect what she thought and felt.

Callie sighed. "I—I just missed you. Wanted to see how you were doing."

She'd missed him? Something banged inside his rib cage, but she remained in the shadows. Hiding from him?

He took a step forward, no longer willing to hide from her. To deprive himself of her.

"I've missed talking to you, too, Callie." He cleared his throat. "Missed you a lot." He looked down and then up at her.

She stepped into the slanted light dappling the straw-covered barn floor. His breath hitched.

Callie was so beautiful. What was wrong with the men in Truelove that she hadn't been claimed long before now? Not that he was in any position to... Jake concentrated on refilling his lungs with oxygen.

It was so good to be able to look at her again. No more quick, surreptitious glances. To drink his fill of her.

Uncertainty dotted her warm brown eyes. "Are you angry with me, Jake?"

He frowned. "Not at all."

Like dust motes in the air, the so-what-is-it-then danced between them.

"I'm no good at relationships, Callie." He ground his teeth. "I failed Tiffany."

"You didn't fail Tiff, Jake. It was Tiff who failed you." Her eyes blazed. "And for the record, you're not the only one with a failure in the love department."

His mouth fell open. "You?" He scowled. "And who?"

A shaft of jealousy twisted him up inside, catching him by surprise.

She tapped her foot on the wooden floor. "Don't sound so surprised that someone might actually find me—"

"I'm not surprised." He clenched his jaw. "You're the most beautiful woman I've ever known…"

She blushed crimson in the universal way of redheads. Jake was coming to the realization he had a thing for redheads. One redhead in particular.

"I'm just surprised I haven't heard about the guy before." He toed the floor with his boot. "Not that you have to tell me anything."

She fluttered her hand. "No point in rehashing how I got dumped."

Jake propped his fists on his hips. "What kind of idiot would jilt you?"

She laughed. "My eighteen-year-old ego wishes you had said that to me all those years ago."

"If I'd been around all those years ago, after I flattened him for ever hurting you, I'd have…" He combed his hand through his hair.

She folded her arms. "Now it's you who's doing the hurting."

Cutting Jake to the quick.

"Try to understand, Callie. I don't want to mess up things with Maisie."

Her chin came up. "Then don't."

She wasn't the only one who could do stubborn. If she wanted honesty, no matter how humiliating, he'd give her honesty.

"I ruin things, Callie. Everything I touch. Everyone I care about." He gulped. "I care too much about you."

"Won't you give us a chance, Jake?" Her eyes beckoned him. "Give me a chance."

Her wistful tone was like relentless drops of water eroding every defense mechanism he erected.

"Caring about someone is always risky." Her mouth pulled downward. "But if you're afraid I'll be like Tiff—"

"You're nothing like Tiffany."

She winced, though he wasn't sure why.

He swiped his hand over his face. "I've not had much success in finding a place of my own, but—"

"Not your fault." She cocked her head. "You've been sabotaged."

"Sabotaged?"

Callie sighed. "You can thank the Truelove matchmakers. They always think they know better than—"

"Maybe they do."

She rocked on the heels of her flats. "What do you mean?"

"Maybe they're right." He gritted his teeth. "Maybe they do know best."

She made an expansive gesture. "Things have moved very fast. Too fast. But don't leave. We can work this out. If nothing else, we can go back to being friends."

He grimaced. "I don't want to be your friend, Callie."

She stiffened. "Oh." And turned to go.

In one stride, he caught her arm. "I mean I don't want to only be your friend. I want…"

She looked at his hand on her arm and then into his eyes. "What do you want, Jake?"

The longing he'd felt but hadn't understood that first day when she'd come out onto the porch resurfaced again. This time with it came something stronger than fear.

"I want to see where this goes with you, Callie."

She placed her hand on his chest. "I'd like that, too, Jake."

The warmth of her hand burned through his flannel shirt. His heart jolted. "And…"

She waited.

"I want to take you to the Apple Festival this weekend."

There. He finally voiced what had been on his mind since he'd spotted the festival poster in town.

She tilted her head. "Are you asking me for a date?"

His heart pounded so hard he feared he might go into cardiac arrest. "If I were to ask you on a date, Callie Jackson, what would you say?" His voice went husky.

"If you were to ask me for a date, Jake McAbee?" Leaning into him, she rose on her tiptoes. "I might have to say yes." Her lips brushed his cheek.

He curled a stray auburn tendril of her hair around his finger. He rubbed the silky lock between his thumb and forefinger before tucking the strand behind the delicate curve of her ear.

Was he doing the right thing? Relationships usually didn't work out for him. Dating Callie was a risk. A huge risk with the potential for total failure. And yet…

"Maisie could be our chaperone." He took her hand. "And I wouldn't mind hearing more about the jerk who broke your heart. Although, his loss, my gain."

"Nothing to tell." She rolled her tongue in her cheek. "Matt didn't break my heart."

He curled his lip. "I've never liked the name Matt."

With a sideways glance, she gave Jake a teasing smile. "So you think we need a chaperone at the Apple Festival?"

To keep from getting ahead of himself again? To prevent him from blurting out his growing feelings for Callie?

"Yes," he whispered, his heart in his voice. "I do."

Chapter Thirteen

Jake had worried what Nash would think of Callie going to the festival with him. He didn't have to wait long to find out. In the barn the next morning as they worked on the tractor, Nash appeared pleased.

"Not a newsflash to me, McAbee. I've seen how your eyes follow my Callie around a room."

Stuffing his hands in the pockets of his jeans, Jake flushed.

"I also see how she looks at you."

His head snapped up. "You think so, sir?"

Tightening the connection, Nash's weathered face brightened. "I'm not too old to remember giving Callie's mom a look like that myself."

"And you're okay with me taking Callie to the festival?"

Turning the wrench, Nash gave the bolt a final twist and straightened. "Sure, especially since you know what a father would do if someone was to hurt his little girl."

"If some moron ever hurt my girl, I'd… I'd…" Jake glowered. "It wouldn't be good. But Maisie's not dating anyone, not until she's at least twenty-five."

Nash used an old rag to wipe the grease from his hands. "Good thing for you, my Callie's over twenty-five, eh?"

"Yes, sir." Jake's mouth curved. "Good thing for me."

A very good thing for him. Other than Maisie, Callie was the best thing that had ever happened to him. He could hardly wait for the festival on Saturday. But he and failure were old friends.

God, please don't let me mess up this chance with Callie.

Saturday morning dawned bright and clear— a perfect autumn mountain day. The air was indeed apple crisp.

He parked his truck in the designated festival parking area. "Wait for me." He came around to open the door for Callie.

Callie's brown eyes sparked. "Such a gentleman."

Taking his arm, she eased out onto the gravel. The touch of her fingers against his skin electrified his pulse.

She must have felt it, too, because her eyebrows lifted. "Static electricity?"

Jake ran his hand down her arm, lacing her fingers in his. "Or not."

Her mouth curved. "Or not."

"Me. Me," Maisie clamored from the car seat.

Letting go of his hand, Callie unfastened the buckles on Maisie's car seat. "Our chaperone is calling."

Callie had braided her hair into a plait that fell to the bottom of her shoulder blades. The elegant pulled-back style wasn't her usual casual look, but allowed him a better view of her face.

She looked so sophisticated he felt a little shy, unused to this side of her. Reminding him there was a lot about Callie he didn't know. Yet, he sensed she'd dressed up for him and their "date."

"My daddy, my daddy." Maisie reached for him as Callie lifted her from the car seat.

If a date included bringing his two-year-old child. And involved throngs of festivalgoers.

"You better take her, Jake." Callie handed Maisie off to him. "She won't be satisfied unless you're within touching distance."

Shifting Maisie on his arm, he clicked the key fob, locking the truck. Holding his daughter was a pleasure that would never fade.

Callie smiled at them. "Last year we used the stroller, but this year—"

"No roller." Maisie's blond curls shook. "Big gull."

Callie stuck her tongue in her cheek. "Good thing we have your daddy, then."

He tickled Maisie's tummy. "You've got your daddy, all right."

Writhing, she giggled. He loved her so much. More than he could have ever imagined.

Lest Callie see the sudden moisture that sprang into his eyes, he planted a raspberry kiss on Maisie's soft little neck, inciting further giggles.

Callie always dressed his daughter in the cutest outfits. Today Maisie wore a tiny blue jean jacket over gray leggings. A large gray cat was embroidered on her long-sleeved pink T-shirt.

"Better get going." He hoisted Maisie high onto his shoulders. "Don't want to miss any of the fun." The street fair was already in full swing.

Wrapping her legs around his neck, he positioned his hands on her small pink cowgirl boots. Maisie placed her hands atop his head as they sailed toward the blocked-off town square. As they wended their way through the crowd, Callie inserted her arm through the crook of his elbow. His pulse jump-started at her nearness.

Town merchants had set up shop on the sidewalks. On the square itself, local artisans manned outdoor booths displaying their colorful handicrafts. The air smelled of barbecue and funnel cakes.

"You'll have to show me the ropes," he whispered in Callie's ear. "I'm the newcomer here." His mouth brushed a silky strand of hair.

A surge of red crept from the collar of her turquoise blouse, but she squeezed his arm.

"Morning, Jake," called a guy Nash had introduced him to at the hardware store. "And aren't you something? Here with some of Truelove's prettiest young ladies…"

Flashing a grin at Callie, Jake broadened his chest. "You've got that right."

And then the gaggle of Truelove matchmakers descended on them.

Miss IdaLee smiled. "Jake."

"Callie…" Miss ErmaJean crowed.

"Good to see y'all here." A significant look from Miss GeorgeAnne. "Together."

"Yes, ma'am." He could practically feel the blush radiating off Callie. Neither of them liked being the center of attention. "Sorry to rush off, but if you ladies would excuse us…"

He moved away toward the stage erected at the end of the square.

"Thanks," Callie whispered.

As if riding a bronco, Maisie bucked on his shoulders. "Pop-Pop." She pointed.

Callie let go of him to hug her father.

Nash winked at him. "I'd offer to look after

Maisie so you two could go have some fun, but all that girl wants is her daddy." He patted Maisie's pink boot, hanging over Jake's shoulder. "Which is exactly as it should be."

Callie nudged Jake as the mayor mounted the steps to the platform. "We're in time for the opening ceremony when Orchard of the Year is awarded."

"Apple Valley should win, of course."

Her cheeks lifted. "Your loyalty is appreciated, but with Dad's illness we didn't enter this year." She took his arm again, and his heart went into overdrive. "Maybe next year."

When an orchard on the other side of the county was announced the winner, Nash broke into cheers.

"One of Dad's oldest friends." Callie glanced at Jake. "A friendly rivalry. One year he wins. Then it's our turn. Both are happy so long as it's one of them."

He threaded his fingers into Callie's. "Definitely yours next year."

She gave him a quick look before a slow, sweet smile spread across her face. He realized he should've clarified he meant the orchard win would be hers next year. But looking into her upturned face, maybe he'd said exactly what he meant.

The woman from church with a fiddle and two men carrying a guitar and a banjo took their places on the stage. And the festival kicked into high gear with strains of bluegrass mountain music.

Maisie's booted heels spurred his chest. "Horsey, horsey."

"She wants to ride the carousel." Callie gestured toward the carnival rides. "She loves the painted ponies."

Promising to reconnect for lunch, they left Nash and headed toward the whirling musical cacophony of the merry-go-round.

Maisie strained forward. "Me. Me."

"Slow down, horse girl." He raised Maisie over his head and set her on the ground.

Maisie lunged.

Callie only just caught her hand. "Wait for our turn, Maisie. The ride has to stop before we get on."

Jake prayed the wonderful ride he was on with his daughter and Callie would never stop. If he could live one perfect day forever, it would be this day with its blue sky and puffy white clouds. Today—for the first time in his life—his heart felt truly complete.

He'd finally found a place to belong. After a long, hard journey, he'd somehow found home.

Jake swallowed the rush of emotion. The carousel ground to a halt. Parents and children exited the ride, and it was their turn to board.

He lifted Maisie onto the platform. "Shouldn't we sit in the carriage?"

Maisie stretched toward a gaily painted, cream-colored palomino. "Big gull. Big gull."

"Nice try." Callie laughed. "But no dice with your *big girl*."

He patted the wooden saddle with the painted replica of an American flag. "She's got good taste."

Callie stepped into the silver stirrup of an adjacent black steed. "Since we've got you this year, I think I'll have a little fun myself." She batted her lashes at him. "And if I wasn't so modest, I'd say Maisie learned her good taste from me."

He hoisted Maisie onto the pony. "Modest and beautiful. All in one package."

Callie's lips curved.

He climbed into the saddle behind his daughter, wrapping his arms around Maisie to keep her secure.

Maisie rocked the stationary pony as if by sheer willpower she could get the carousel spinning. "Big gull."

"Not too big, too fast." He nuzzled his nose in her hair. "Be Daddy's baby for a little while longer? Okay?"

"'Kay, my daddy."

He placed her hands around the center metal pole. "Hold on tight, baby girl."

"Maisie! Maisie!"

Ahead of them in the curve of the platform, Amber's girls waved. One of the twins sat astride a roaring tiger, and the other rode a giraffe.

Standing between the preschoolers, Amber smiled. "Hey, y'all."

There was a sudden shudder. With a whir of gears, the carousel began to move. Callie grabbed on to her own pole. Amber steadied herself between her girls.

When her pony began to glide up and down, Maisie gasped. But over her shoulder, she threw her father a happy grin. He tightened his hold around her middle, relishing the opportunity to hold her close.

As the merry-go-round picked up speed, a carnival tune lilted from the calliope. Shrieks of delight erupted around them. Callie smiled over at him. "It never gets old."

Nor did being with Callie and Maisie.

The calliope wound into an old carnival tune he recognized. But instead of *K-K-K-Katy*, he changed the words to fit the small person in his arms. And in his heart.

Bending, he whisper-sang into her ear. "'M-M-M-Maisie, beautiful Maisie. You're the only g-g-g-girl that I adore.'"

Maisie didn't let go of the pole, but she nestled the crown of her head against his chest.

"'When the m-m-m-moon shines over the cowshed—'"

Breaking off, he grinned at the bemused smile on Callie's face. "Gotta love those farm girls."

She laughed so hard she almost unseated herself, but she quickly repositioned her grip on the pole.

"May-zee song." Maisie elbowed him. "My daddy."

He took up where he left off. "'I'll be waiting at the k-k-k-kitchen door...'"

Callie let go of the pole long enough to clap. The ride slowed to a crawl and then to a standstill. After dismounting, he plucked Maisie off the pony and offered his hand to Callie.

She swung her leg over, but stumbled into him. "Haven't quite got my carousel legs back this season."

The twins raced over. Amber's blue eyes held a smile. "Has Callie taken you to see her photography exhibit at the town hall yet?"

He arched his eyebrow, and Callie dropped her gaze. "Why no, Amber, she has not. I had no idea, in fact, that she'd entered a photography exhibit. Although, I'm not surprised, seeing that she's so talented."

"I'm not—"

"She is extremely talented." Amber took firm hold of her daughters' hands. "Everyone wants Callie to do their wedding photos or family portraits."

Callie stepped off the platform, making way

for other families to get on. "It's not that big of a deal."

With Maisie in his arms, he joined her. "More modesty?"

"Callie studied photography at college before she came home." Amber caught his eye. "She's always wanted to open her own studio."

"Amber..." Callie glared.

Dragging their mother with them, the twins jumped to the ground in a move worthy of a paratrooper.

"Why don't you two head there now?" Amber let go of her daughters and flipped her hair over her shoulder. "Let me take our girls to the playground. They can work off some energy, and you can enjoy the photos."

Callie shook her head. "I don't think—"

"I think that's a fabulous idea." He widened his stance. "And thank you so much, Amber, for this invaluable information that Callie failed to mention."

"Yeah." Callie clenched her jaw. "Thank you so much, Amber."

Smirking, Amber turned toward Maisie. "Want to come with us to the school playground, Maisie?"

Maisie's arm tightened a fraction around his neck. "My daddy?" Lip protruding, she cut her eyes to Callie. "Cawee?"

Amber patted Maisie's cowgirl boot. "Callie

and your daddy are going to look at some pictures."

He hugged Maisie close, her sweet baby smell tickling his nostrils. "We won't be gone long, Maisie. You go have fun with the girls."

Nodding, she wriggled, and he put her down. The girls each took one of Maisie's hands.

Amber herded the children toward the far end of Main Street. "Take your time," she called.

For the first time that day, they were finally alone.

He'd never been good at the dating thing, much less relationships, but with Callie it felt right.

Jake held out his hand. "I want to see your photos."

She gave him a lopsided smile. "You may live to regret that."

"I won't. Although—" he jerked his chin toward the carousel "—I may have spoken too soon."

Crinkling her eyes, she took his hand. "About what?"

His gaze bored into hers. "Maisie's not the only girl I'm coming to adore."

Chapter Fourteen

The closer they came to the town hall, the more nervous Callie became. Only Jake's warm, work-calloused hand in hers prevented her from making a getaway. Her *Faces of the Mountain* series was different from her usual work.

She was only just now venturing beyond brides and families. Stretching herself and her craft, she'd tried to capture not only images but also what it meant to live in the Blue Ridge Mountains. To convey what her mountain home meant to her. Suppose Jake didn't get the pictures? Or, worse, didn't like them?

At the courthouse steps, he paused. "I like your hair like that."

She tucked a tendril of dangling hair behind her ear. "Thank you."

Blue as a Carolina morning, his eyes followed the movement of her hand. "But I like your hair however you wear it."

Her pulse jerked.

A muscle ticked in his jaw. "I think you have the most beautiful hair I've ever seen."

"Thank you, Jake." Swallowing, she reached to brush a strand of hair out of her face, but he beat her to it.

"May I?"

She nodded, her heart clanging almost painfully against her rib cage. He rolled the wisp of hair between his fingers before gently feathering it behind her ear.

He dropped his hand. "We should go inside." His voice had gone husky, thrilling her that being near her could affect him so.

She'd begun to believe love had forever passed her by. Until Jake McAbee arrived at the orchard.

Inside the town hall, reluctantly she turned him toward the exhibit containing her framed photographs.

She'd never liked anyone as much as Jake, and, other than her father, never admired a man so much. She teared up on a daily basis seeing the way he was with Maisie.

Putting Maisie to bed each night. Singing sweet little tunes in his rusty baritone she suspected he made up as he went along. Like on the carousel.

Was he the one God had planned for her from the beginning? If so, she was thankful for not only the good gift of Maisie, but for Jake, as well.

If she wasn't very careful, she would find herself completely— She sighed. Who was she kidding?

Amber was right. She did have it bad. Bad for an ex-soldier daddy with the most loving heart of any man she'd ever known.

He let go of her hand as he studied the pictures. Stepping back a pace to better examine her photos, he fingered the cleft in his chin. Twisting her stomach into additional knots.

She searched his features, anxious to know his opinion. The cleft in his chin melted her into a chocolate puddle. Everything about Jake McAbee liquefied her insides.

Avoiding him had been excruciating as she'd agonized over pursuing a relationship with a man from whom she was keeping secrets. Yet, in the end, she couldn't let the possibility of what they could mean to each other slip from her grasp.

So she'd decided to tell him the truth about Tiff. Even though it would hurt him. Though it meant he might never trust Callie again. She had to take the chance.

Feeling the way she did about him, she could no longer withhold the truth. A real, lasting relationship shouldn't be based on secrets. Wouldn't survive secrets.

"I can't decide which I like the best." He cocked his head. "*Autumn's Splendor. Winter's Solace. Spring's Rebirth.* Or *Summer's Resonance.*" He reached for her hand. "You are very talented. Are there other photos of home you could show me?"

Her galloping heart slowed to a canter. He'd said, "Home." He got it. He got her.

"I don't have much time for photography. With Dad, the orchard and Maisie—"

"But I'm here now. I can help you. You deserve more time to do what you love."

"I love the orchard, Dad and Maisie, too." She let her shoulders rise and fall. "Other than the occasional paying client, this is a hobby."

He put his hands on his hips. "It doesn't have to be a hobby, Callie. Good gifts shouldn't be wasted. And you shouldn't waste yours."

She needed to find the right time to share Tiff's secret. To trust his love for Maisie. But not today. Nothing should be allowed to mar this perfect day.

But in the future, when their relationship was stronger…when she found the courage…and the words. Soon, she promised herself.

"You do so much for everyone else." He ran his thumb over her hand. "I just want you to be happy."

She looked into his eyes. "I am happy, Jake."

Callie couldn't remember ever being happier.

She was so incredibly happy it stole her breath. Her dad was well. She had Maisie. And Jake McAbee had come into her life. The past few years of her life, she'd been marking time. Holding her breath. Waiting for someone like him to find her.

Like the story Maisie loved so much, *Sleeping Beauty*, who'd waited for her prince to come into her tower—orchard bower in Callie's case—and awaken her to life again.

Only thing missing from Callie's story—the kiss.

He bit the inside of his cheek. "The Apple Festival may not have been the best idea for a date."

She blinked. "The festival isn't a good date?"

"Not when the only thing I can think about..." His Adam's apple bobbed in his throat.

"What are you thinking about, Jake?" she whispered.

He ran his hand over his head. "All I'm thinking about is where I can kiss you."

Callie's heart pounded. "Not when?" Because *when* was the only thing on her mind.

"The *when* depends on the lady."

She looked at him. "This lady says there's no time like the present."

His arms slipped around her waist. "I like the way you think."

Callie arched her eyebrow. "I think we've waited long e—"

Swooping, his lips found hers. But almost as quickly he drew back, giving her the freedom to break away if she wished. Callie didn't wish.

Instead, her hands traveled across his broad

back and interlocked behind his neck. She pulled his head toward her mouth.

"Callie..." he murmured before his lips claimed hers again.

Kissing him, she reminded herself to breathe. He held her so gently, like a precious china tea-cup. She felt so cherished with him. Safe.

What she wanted him to feel, too. That with her, he'd found a safe place. A place where he belonged. That with her, he'd always feel as if he'd come home.

Applause broke out around them. They sprang apart. They'd acquired an audience.

Miss GeorgeAnne sniffed. "About time."

"Well done." Miss ErmaJean's fist pumped the air.

Miss IdaLee placed her hand to her throat. "I was beginning to think I wouldn't live to see the day."

Callie flushed to the roots of her hair, but Jake didn't let her drift far. He held on to her, his arm pressing her against his side. He gave Callie that crooked, one-sided smile, which invariably made her weak in the knees.

She licked her lip. Spearmint. Jake McAbee tasted like green spearmint gum.

"Don't let us interrupt." IdaLee gestured.

"Carry on," GeorgeAnne urged.

"Pretend we're not here." ErmaJean fluttered.

He hugged Callie. "You're not. I will. Don't mind if I do."

But five was definitely a crowd. "Jake..."

He laughed and pulled her toward the exit. "Rain check?"

Reaching the town hall lobby, she stopped him. "Would you look at that?" Her hand on his chest, through the fabric of his flannel shirt she felt his heartbeat accelerate. "Is that a rain cloud I see there in the sky?"

He smiled. "Rain cloud?" He pretended to peer through the glass-paned door. "Are you sure?"

Stretching on the tips of her toes, she leaned into him. "I'm sure. It's forecast." She tilted her chin. "I've always loved the rain." Her lips parted.

His breath ruffled the lock of hair at her earlobe. "Then I say, let it pour."

Jake smiled against her lips as he kissed her again.

But with people trying to enter the building, this kiss was far too brief. He drew her outside onto the sidewalk. "Wonder what Maisie is doing."

"Probably wondering what we're doing."

They ambled down the sidewalk. "Shall we tell her?"

She blushed again. "Jake."

He grinned.

She swatted at him. "Stop teasing."

He tucked her hand into his, where it belonged.

Passing The Mason Jar, he cocked his head. "You were going to tell me more about this Matt person."

She rolled her eyes. "That's not how I remember it."

"You were going to tell me about this emotionally deficient jerk who was too stupid to see Truelove's greatest treasure."

She pursed her lips. "A treasure, am I, then?"

His quiet smile reduced her to a quivery puddle of gelatin. "You are to me. And Maisie."

She didn't have the heart to tease him anymore. "His name is Matt Fleming."

"Matt—" Jake's eyes widened. "As in Amber?"

"Amber's older brother. Soldier, tough like you. When he graduated high school, he joined the Marines and that was the end of us."

Jake snorted. "Army beats jarheads any day of the week, sweetheart."

Ignoring the interservice rivalry—and to satisfy her curiosity—she gave Jake a quick peck on the cleft in his chin. "Looks like I prefer soldiers. Go army."

Laughter rumbled in his chest. "That's my girl."

She liked—no, she loved—the sound of that.

At a picnic table under the Kiwanis awning, they found her father, Amber and the children eating foot-long hot dogs.

Her dad waved a french fry. "Figured you two would join us sooner or later."

Crawling over Pop-Pop, Maisie plopped herself in "my daddy's" lap. Jake pulled Callie next to him on the bench. Keeping her close.

Her father and Amber exchanged amused glances, but she was so happy Jake was a part of her life she didn't care who knew.

After lunch Amber and her girls headed off for more carnival rides. Callie wanted to peruse the handicrafts for sale, but Maisie wanted to get her face painted.

Jake motioned Callie toward the street fair. "You enjoy yourself for a change. We'll find you."

"Are you sure?"

"Me be kitty." Maisie captured his cheeks between her small palms. "My daddy, too."

He shot Callie a wry look. "What have I gotten myself into now?"

She toyed with the end of her braid. "Last year Maisie insisted my face be painted with butterflies and flowers."

His mouth dropped. "Seriously?"

"Better you than me, McAbee." Nash twirled a toothpick in his mouth. "What a parent will do for their child, eh?"

With an air of exaggerated martyrdom, Jake set Maisie on her feet and took her hand. "Let's go, Maisie."

She bounced on the sidewalk. "Yay, my daddy! Yay spawkle! Yay gwitter!"

He groaned, but his smile belied his protests.

"Never let it be said I left any man to deal with face painting alone." Nash took Maisie's other hand. "I got your six, soldier."

"Much appreciated." Jake's eyes darted to Callie. "Enjoy yourself, you hear?"

She gave him a two-fingered salute. "Aye-aye, Ensign."

He shook his head. "That's the navy, Callie."

Nash slapped his shoulder. "Plenty of time to reeducate her, son."

Jake saluted her back. "Challenge accepted."

Roaming through the vendor booths, Callie did enjoy herself. She stopped to talk with one of her mother's potter friends. She lingered at the metalworker's stall, delighting in the whimsy of the whirligigs. Someone bumped into her.

Callie staggered. "I'm sorry I—"

A rough hand shoved her into the small alley between the hardware store and the post office. Stumbling, she fell into the brick wall.

"You're going to be sorry, all right," the man growled.

Her head snapped up.

And despite everything she'd done to prevent this disastrous moment from happening, standing in front of Callie was her worst nightmare come true.

Chapter Fifteen

Brandon Lloyd towered over her, cutting her off from the throng of festivalgoers beyond the alley. "Long time no see, Callie."

She shivered. "Not long enough."

He'd cleaned up his appearance since the last time she'd seen him. In high school Brandon had been the leader of a pack of delinquents. He'd enticed Tiff to run away with him to Atlanta. Years later it was to him she'd returned when she left Jake.

Now, with his auburn hair neatly trimmed and his face clean-shaven, Brandon appeared fairly respectable. Like a young IT guy or accountant. But the overpowering stench of his expensive cologne made her want to gag.

To look at him in his rust-colored button-down shirt and khakis, no one would ever guess what a loathsome creep he was. But Callie had known from the beginning. Tiff had discovered this for herself only after a great deal of anguish.

Callie never understood what Tiff found so alluring in Brandon Lloyd. But he was good at what he did—conning people for a living. And Tiff had fallen for him, hook, line and sinker.

He sold illusions and once he'd emptied a mark's coffers of everything, he skipped town. In high school he'd been a small-time drug dealer. When Tiff became his girlfriend, he was the one who introduced her to drugs.

Brandon Lloyd, the ultimate lowlife.

He threw her a despicable look. "I believe you have something that belongs to me."

"I don't know what you're talking about." She pushed past him.

Brandon shoved her deeper into the deserted alley. "I believe you do."

Heart thudding, she gazed over his shoulder toward the sounds of laughter and music filtering into the alley. Anything to avoid looking into his eyes. The moss green eyes that had so mesmerized Tiff repulsed Callie.

"I want my kid."

Callie's mouth went dry. "She's not your child."

"Sure, she is." His lips twisted. "You know it. I know it."

"No." She shook her head so hard some of her hair fell out of her braid. "It's not true. The birth certificate—"

"Doesn't matter whose name is on the birth certificate." His eyes beaded on Callie. "She's my kid, and I want her."

The hope Callie had nurtured since meeting Jake was crushed under the weight of Tiff's affinity for lying and his absolute conviction. Brandon—not Jake—was Maisie's biological father. How she'd longed with all her heart for that not to be true. What she'd feared, but blindly refused to believe. But perhaps she could convince Brandon to see reason. If he cared anything about his child…

She scanned his face. "Maisie's happy at the farm. What would you want with a child in your life? She'd only be a hindrance to your… to your…"

"My what?" Brandon sneered.

She touched her throat. "Your activities."

He cocked his head as if considering the idea. Then his mouth hardened. "But a sweet little girl like Maisie—" it made her want to retch hearing Maisie's name on his lips "—could bring new business opportunities my way."

Violating her rule about staying as far away from Brandon as humanly possible, she seized his arm. "Please, Brandon. Don't."

His eyes gleamed.

"I'll do anything." Panic nearly blinded Callie. "Please don't take her away. Jake—"

"Yeah." Brandon curled his lip. "I've seen her around town with her fake dad."

Fear coiled in Callie's belly. How long had Brandon been watching them?

"Never figured you had it in you, Jackson." His gaze shone with admiration. "Quite a con you've got going." Brandon smirked. "Convincing G.I. Joe that the kid is his. Getting him to pony up."

"It's not a con." Callie opened her hands. "Jake is her father."

Brandon snorted. He motioned toward the square. "You want me to call a deputy? 'Cause I've got nothing but time and the law on my side."

She stared at him in horror. This couldn't be happening.

"You want me to take a paternity test?" he growled. "I'll head right over to the clinic." He got in her face. She cringed. "Soon as you tell that poor army chump that you've been trying to pass off another man's child as his."

On her deathbed, Tiff had made Callie promise to never allow Brandon to get anywhere near Maisie. Since Jake's name was on the birth certificate, Callie had hoped—prayed—that for once Tiff had told the truth. That Jake was truly Maisie's father.

But she'd refused to allow Callie to contact

him and let him know about Maisie. *After I'm gone*, Tiff had said. *Tell him I'm sorry.*

Was it guilt? Fear? So many things about Tiff, Callie had never understood.

But she'd understood the need to protect an innocent child from the likes of Brandon Lloyd. How could she allow this monster to take Maisie into his sordid world? And what about Jake? Her legs almost went out from under her, imagining with sickening clarity the devastation he would feel.

After a lifetime of hurt and rejection, learning the truth would destroy him. She couldn't let that happen. She wouldn't let that happen. He and Maisie needed each other.

Pushing against the rough brick, she straightened. No matter what it took, she wasn't going to allow Brandon to tear them apart.

"What do you really want, Brandon? Because I know it isn't the chance to play daddy. You want money?" She rolled her eyes. "Of course you want money. All you've ever cared about is money. How much will it take to make you go away and leave us alone?"

His face broadened into a disgusting grin. "How much do you have? How much is Maisie's life and G.I. Joe's happiness worth to you?"

Anything. Everything. She'd rather die than see Jake and Maisie separated. And in that moment she realized how much she loved Jake McAbee.

She folded her arms. "How much, Brandon?"

"I think five thousand dollars might do it."

She gasped.

Brandon wrinkled his nose. "Too much to keep you from losing your baby? Too much to save that happy little family thing you got going?"

How in the world would she find that amount of money? But she would. She had no choice.

She jutted out her jaw. "And if I give you the money, you won't contact us again? Ever again?"

"Why, sure, sweetheart." That oily smile of his. "If that's what you want. Although Tiff found me—"

She shoved him away.

He shrugged. "To each his own. I'm renting a trailer out on High Rock Road. The old Morgan place. Meet me there on Monday at five o'clock with the money."

Monday. So soon, but what choice did she have?

He smoothed the front of his shirt. "And if you don't show up, my next visit will be to break the news to G.I. Joe that he's been duped." He moved aside.

Rushing past, she staggered out of the alley. For a moment the activity, the noise, the sights, overwhelmed her senses. She'd taken no more than two tottering steps before a hand cupped her elbow.

Callie reared, wrenching free.

"Whoa!" Maisie's arms around his neck, Jake stepped back. "I thought you saw us." His gaze flicked toward the alley.

Suppose Brandon saw Maisie and decided to confront Jake?

"What were you doing—"

She yanked him away from the alley and toward the cheerful street-fair traffic. She wondered if she looked as shaken as she felt.

"Are you okay?" He stopped on the sidewalk in front of the pawnshop. "What's wrong?"

"Nothing's wrong." But trembling, she let go of him, wrapping her arms around herself. "You just surprised me." She unfolded her arms. "That's all."

"Meow, Cawee." Maisie pushed her face at Callie. "See me?"

Callie fought the fear mushrooming inside her head. "What?" She took a steady breath, hoping neither Jake nor Maisie noticed her agitation.

"The face paint." His brow creasing, Jake feathered back the clump of hair that had fallen across Callie's eyes.

Unable to meet his gaze, she held out her arms for Maisie and hugged her close, grateful for the calming warmth of her little body.

"Meow, Cawee."

The face-paint artist had drawn whiskers across Maisie's cheeks and a pink triangle on the tip of her nose.

"Who is this cute creature, Jake?" She pretended to frown. "Who is this little kitty cat? What's happened to our Maisie?"

"Meow." Maisie clawed the air.

"What about me?" Jake turned his head, giving her a good look at the broad black and orange stripes across his cheeks. "Am I cute, too, Callie Rose?" He winked.

Maisie laughed. "My daddy not coot."

"Papa Cat's not supposed to be cute. Papa Cat is ferocious." Growling, Jake tickled her tummy. She giggled in Callie's arms.

He kissed the top of Maisie's head. "Only ferocious when it comes to keeping his pretty kitty safe."

Callie was never certain how she managed to get through the rest of the day. Maisie fell asleep in the truck on the ride home. Humming a tune, Jake reached across the seat for Callie's hand.

Guilt and dread in equal measure surged in her heart. If he ever found out how she'd deceived him, he'd never forgive her. He'd never look at her the same way again. He'd never fall in love with her.

She'd already fallen as hard, long and fast as she could for him. But it was up to her to ensure he didn't lose Maisie and that her tenuous relationship with Jake wasn't ruined forever.

The consequences of losing either of them were too terrible to contemplate. She didn't sleep that night. How could she keep Brandon from destroying their lives?

Sensing her disquiet at church the next morning, both Jake and her dad cast anxious looks her way. She made excuses when they asked if anything was wrong.

But if she didn't confide in someone she was going to explode, so that afternoon she called Amber and asked if she could drop by.

Her dad was engrossed in a football game on television. Jake and Maisie had gone for a tractor ride in the orchard. With the high school kids manning the store, she slipped away to Amber's small house on the outskirts of town.

Amber met her outside on the rickety porch. It hurt Callie's heart to see how Amber and the girls were living—barely surviving in this decrepit, run-down shack. The yard consisted of packed dirt. Yet, because of Amber's pride, there was no use in offering to help.

"What's up?" Amber sank onto the top step, arms wrapped around her legs to keep out the chill.

Callie made a mental note to buy Amber a new winter coat for Christmas. Everything Amber earned on her meager salary at The Mason Jar went to food, school, rent for this slum dwelling and gas for her car.

"Where are the twins?"

"Long day at the festival yesterday." Amber

brought her knees to her chest. "The girls are asleep, or I'd say let's go inside and get out of the cold."

That wasn't the real reason Amber didn't invite Callie indoors, but she allowed her friend her pride-saving excuse.

Amber's house wasn't their usual meeting place. She didn't like her friends to see the stark reality of her hardship. But today was an emergency. Brandon's timetable was like a ticking bomb in the back of Callie's mind. Swallowing past the bile, Callie eased down beside her.

"Looks like you had a great day yesterday." When she didn't respond, Amber elbowed her. "The best kind of day."

"Brandon wants Maisie…" Callie burst into tears.

When she calmed down enough to be coherent, she poured out the rest of the story. Her promise to Tiff. Her desperation to keep Maisie safe. To prevent this very thing from happening.

"And Jake…" Callie broke into a fresh round of sobs.

"You must tell him the truth." Amber kept her arm around Callie's shoulders. "Everything."

"I—I can't. He'd be crushed. Feel so betrayed."

Amber shook her head. "I can't believe you kept this from everyone. This isn't like you, Callie. Why all this time—"

"Maisie's better off with Jake." Callie raised

her chin. "And I was going to tell him." Moisture flooded her eyes, blurring her vision. "I just hadn't gotten around to it."

Amber blew out a breath. "The truth has a habit of coming out, Callie. You know that. And at the worst possible time. Now is your chance to come clean about Brandon and Tiff, to get ahead of this before disaster strikes. Jake will know how to handle this."

Callie wrested free. "I can't tell him and risk…" She bit her lip.

Amber tilted her head. "And risk him never trusting you again?"

Callie stiffened. "If I just give Brandon the money… You remember how he is."

Amber's mouth thinned. "Brandon Lloyd is an absolute snake. I wouldn't trust him—and neither should you—as far as I could throw him. Who's to say that once he gets the money, he won't come back for more?" She frowned. "The insatiable greed. A blackmailer never gets enough."

Callie combed her fingers through her hair. "I—I can't think about that right now. I just have to get through this crisis."

"Where will you get hold of that kind of money by tomorrow?"

"I've racked my brain… I'll empty out my bank account." Callie lowered her gaze, toeing her boot into the wooden step. "Pawn the camera."

Amber gasped. "You bought the camera with

the money your mom set aside in her will for your dreams."

Callie raised her shoulders and let them drop. "You're a mother, Amber. Blood or not, I'm the only mother Maisie has ever known. Wouldn't you do that and more if it meant protecting your girls from someone like Brandon?"

Amber pursed her lips. "Blood or not, Jake McAbee would never allow a man like Brandon to get within ten feet of Maisie or you. You have to tell him. And your father."

Callie tossed her hair over her shoulder. "My father is only now getting back to where he was before the pneumonia. I won't saddle him with this burden. This was my mess, and I have to be the one to clean it up."

Amber stood so abruptly Callie fell against the railing. "Lying on that hard bed you've made for yourself? You sound like my father. I think you're making a mistake. You're wrong about Jake. It isn't only him who has trust issues."

Gripping the handrail, Callie rose. "It has to be this way, Amber."

"I don't like the idea of you meeting Brandon alone. The trailer he's renting is in the middle of nowhere." Amber set her jaw. "Who's to say what else he may have in mind?" Her mouth tightened. "Anything could happen and there'd be no one to stop him."

"Pray for me, then."

Amber's eyes narrowed. "Did you pray before you made this deal with Brandon Lloyd?"

She'd made so many mistakes since Tiff had arrived on her doorstep, sick and pregnant. Callie wasn't sure God wanted to hear from her anymore. And she didn't blame Him.

Callie felt as vile as Brandon, perhaps even more contemptible because the culmination of her deception had the potential to destroy someone whose happiness had become dearer to Callie than her own.

She scrubbed her forehead. "I should go."

Amber caught her hand. "I'll pray that you will be safe. And that God will bring beauty out of the brokenness." Through a haze of tears, Amber smiled at her. "He's good at that, you know."

Callie wasn't sure how anything good could come from the lies Tiff had told, or the cover-up to which Callie had been an accessory. But if anyone could bring beauty out of this chaos, it would be God.

Considering the mess she'd made of everything, it would have to be God.

Jake wasn't sure what was wrong, but sometime between visiting the photography exhibit and the end of the festival something had changed with Callie.

Late afternoon on Monday he parked the truck in front of the hardware store and got out. He'd volunteered to go into town to buy the PVC pipe, giving himself time to process what had transpired between him and Callie on Saturday and to ponder what had been going on with Callie since then.

She'd been aloof. Brooding. When he and Maisie returned from riding the tractor Sunday afternoon, she'd been gone. Visiting Amber, she'd said, but from the troubled look in her eyes, he was sure there was something more going on.

Now, equally distracted, he roamed the store aisles. Something had happened between their kiss and when they'd reconnected after face painting. Thinking about the kiss, he halted in front of the display of plumbing supplies.

The kiss had been spectacular.

Or at least, spectacular for him. Yet, unlike Tiffany, Callie wore her every emotion on her beautiful face. She couldn't have kissed him like she did if she hadn't felt the same.

Surely, he hadn't misread her signals. He'd given her the opportunity to break it off if she wanted, but she hadn't wanted to. Instead, she'd wanted to kiss him again.

The second kiss had been at her initiative, he reminded himself. No self-doubting. Callie had been clear how she felt about him and pursuing a relationship.

He glanced at his watch. On Maisie duty, Nash would be wondering what was keeping him. Callie had disappeared right after lunch to run errands.

Jake frowned. She'd run errands that morning, but she must have forgotten to do something in town. He sorted through the box on the shelf, looking for the plastic elbow joint he needed.

He hadn't believed it possible, but God had given him another chance at love. Him, Jake McAbee, who'd messed up so badly with Tiffany. But he knew beyond a shadow of doubt God had meant for him to reunite with his daughter. And part of His plan had included finding Callie.

Callie was a great and wonderful gift to him from the Father. Like no father he'd ever known before, a father worth trusting. A father who'd brought Jake home to Truelove—a place of belonging.

Jake shuffled toward the checkout counter.

He was incredibly grateful and humbled that God had given him Maisie and Callie to love. And thankful that Maisie loved him. He didn't know if he'd ever get over God's blessings to him. Much more than he deserved.

One day—he breathed a prayer as he handed money over to the cashier—one day, God willing, Callie would love him, too.

No use in denying his feelings—he was in love with Callie Jackson. Deeply, irrevocably in love. He'd never imagined love could be like this, that he could feel such settled contentment just by being with her. Life with Tiffany during the short months of their marriage had been turbulent, full of anxiety and a raking inadequacy.

Stuffing the receipt in the bag, he stumbled onto the sidewalk. He got only a few feet before he had to stop and blink, allowing his eyes time to adjust to the midafternoon glare of the sun.

Callie was nothing like Tiffany, thank God. She was loyal, honest and good. His heart—like Maisie's—was safe in her hands. She'd never be disloyal. She'd never betray him. His heart had found its home with Callie.

So he had to do things right this time. No rushing. With everything out in the open, above reproach. Protective of Callie and her good name, he intended to honor her by pursuing their relationship in a God-honoring way.

Vision clearing, he found himself in front of the pawnshop. Staring at a camera with assorted lenses on display behind the plate glass window. It looked like—

Squinting, he pressed his face close to the glass. The specially ordered camera strap. How many custom denim camera straps were there in Truelove, North Carolina? He guessed not many.

Why was Callie's camera in the pawnshop? She'd taken a few photos Saturday morning before they left for the festival. The pawnshop, like many stores in Truelove, was closed on Sunday. She had to have brought the camera here today. What was going on? She loved her camera. Why would she have sold it?

His gut clenched. Was this about Nash? Were there medical bills Jake wasn't aware of? The orchard was coming out of a couple of years of bad harvests. He raked his hand over his head. Why hadn't they said something?

Jake had money in the bank. From a time when he had nothing and no one to spend it on. He would be glad to help them—not that the Jacksons would ever ask. They wouldn't have to ask. He'd offer, and not take no for an answer.

They'd taken care of his daughter for over two years. And they were his friends. He swallowed. Perhaps soon they'd become family. He stepped into the pawnshop. He wouldn't allow Callie to sacrifice her dreams anymore.

Emerging with the reclaimed camera equipment in a tote bag, he was surprised to find Amber waiting outside on the sidewalk.

He lifted the bag. "Did you know about this? What's going on?"

"I'm so glad I found you." Amber grabbed his arm. "Nash said you were at the hardware store but…"

He staggered. "Maisie?"

"No, Jake. Maisie's fine." Amber chewed her lip. "I can't believe she actually sold the camera to pay him. Have you heard from Callie lately?"

His heart hammered. "Not since— Why? What's wrong with Callie? Why does she need money?"

Amber closed her eyes. "So stubborn. Too trusting. I told her."

"What's going on? Where is Callie? Tell me," he grunted.

"She didn't want you to know, but I made her promise to text me when she left him, but I haven't heard from her. I'm worried."

"Him who? Matt?"

"Matt? He's in Afghanistan. Why would she— Never mind." She fluttered her hand. "We have to find her before it's too late."

His heart skipped a beat.

"She's done something foolish, Jake." Amber squeezed his arm. "But I promise you, she did it out of love."

"Who does she owe money to, Amber?"

"Brandon's dangerous." Amber's large blue eyes sharpened. "And I'm afraid, Jake. I'm really afraid this time she's in way over her head."

Chapter Sixteen

The overhanging tree canopy on the heavily rutted drive obliterated what little light remained in the day. Night fell swiftly in the mountains. Already the shadows were long.

Callie rounded a bend and glanced into the rearview mirror. The forest had swallowed her, cutting her off completely from the paved secondary road.

She stopped her car in front of the trailer on the old Morgan farm. Amber's little house was a palace compared to this. Car parts and rusted automobiles littered the yard.

As she climbed out of the car, a bleak wind whistled from the ridge, chilling Callie to the bone. Clutching the paper sack, she closed the door with a click.

She'd emptied her meager savings account, which, after a few years of local event photography, had just begun to exhibit a healthy balance. But it hadn't been enough.

After leaving the bank this morning, her next stop had been the pawnshop. Walking away from her camera had felt like severing a limb. Worse. The camera had been her mother's last gift to her. An affirmation that life still held wonderful promise for Callie. But it had to be done.

Anything to keep Maisie with Jake. To prevent Jake from ever learning that his beloved child wasn't his. He'd been through enough. If it was within her power, she vowed to spare him from this last final blow.

The trailer door opened with a menacing screech. She flinched. Catching sight of her, Brandon's long, freckled face widened into a grin, a caricature of a normal person's smile.

At the top of the steps, he motioned. "Come in, come in."

Said the spider to the fly.

Callie shivered. "I'll stay right here, thank you." She leaned against the car, taking a measure of comfort from the clicking sounds of the cooling engine.

"You have what we discussed?" His eyes narrowed. "What you and Tiff owe me?"

She held out the bag.

Coming off the porch, he crossed over to her and snatched the bag out of her hand. "Is it all here?"

She lifted her chin. "Count it, if you don't believe me."

"I will." Brandon rummaged through the cash. "Tiff's already stiffed me once."

Callie's gaze flitted to the trailer. "Quite the comedown from the condo Tiff described in Atlanta."

His hands stilled. "Thanks to you, my fortune is about to change." Raising his head, he took a step closer.

Backing against the hood of her car, she clenched her teeth to prevent them from chattering. She mustn't let him sense her fear. Like a predator cat—one of the few creatures in the animal kingdom who didn't hunt only for food—Brandon liked to toy with his victims before devouring them.

"If—if..." She cleared her throat. "If we're finished here, I'll be on my way." She groped behind her for the car handle.

When he lunged, she screamed.

His hand clamping around her wrist, he hauled her away from the car. "I think it's time to discuss the next payment."

"Let go of me." She tried jerking free. "You said this would be the end of it."

He twisted her arm, and she cried out again. "How much is my silence worth to you, Callie? You told me you'd do anything to keep G.I. Joe from learning the truth. What does anything look like to you?"

She beat at his torso for all the good it did. She'd made a terrible mistake in coming here. Black dots spiraled before her eyes. She felt herself stumbling as the ground rose to meet her, but she couldn't lose consciousness, not now.

God, help me. I should've never—

When Jake's truck came barreling out of the woods down the drive, Brandon froze. And she broke away.

The truck—with Amber's frightened face also inside—screeched to a stop beside her car. Dust swirled. Coughing, Callie hurled herself toward them.

Brandon sprinted after her, but Jake flew out of the truck and threw himself between them. Amber scrambled out, and Callie ran into her arms. Suddenly, the twilight of evening was filled with the sound of sirens and flashing blue lights. Two Truelove police cruisers came to a halt.

The officers piled out, one catching hold of Jake's raised fist. The other policeman wrestled Brandon to the ground. Brandon writhed, but the officer yanked his hands behind his back and cuffed him.

"Last week we got word from the Georgia State Police that you might be headed this way."

The younger officer smirked. "Been looking for you ever since."

The older officer eyed Jake. "If I let go of you, you're going to calm down, right?"

Jake nodded, and the officer dropped his hold on Jake's forearm. "You okay, Miss Jackson?"

"Yes," she rasped. The policeman was an old friend of her father's.

The other officer yanked Brandon upright. "This will be the last clean air you breathe for decades. You've got charges against you a mile long and in three states."

She turned her face away as Brandon yelled curses at them.

"We'll need to get a statement from all of you." Her father's police friend leaned against his cruiser. "Come to the station tomorrow when you get the chance." That was small-town law enforcement.

"Thank You, God, we got here in time." Tears ran down Amber's cheeks. "I called the police on the way here. We were so afraid…"

Callie put her hand on her throat. "You—you told Jake?"

"Only that you were in danger." Amber wiped her eyes. "If I hadn't—"

For a second Callie flailed as someone pulled her away from Amber, but she found herself pressed against Jake's coat. Inhaling his spicy scent, she relaxed.

"Are you all right?" Jake's voice rumbled. "I'd have never found this place without Amber's help. Why were you paying this monster?"

"I'm sorry, Callie," Amber whispered. "I didn't know what else to do to save you."

"Callie's here to buy my child," Brandon hooted.

Jake's hands tightened on her upper arms. "What's he talking about, Callie?" he growled.

Please, God, no. Don't let him find out this—

"I don't care whose name is on the birth certificate," Brandon shouted. "Tiff left Atlanta with my brat in her belly, and that kid's mine. I've got rights."

Going ramrod stiff, Jake thrust Callie from him. "Maisie's my little girl…" His gaze darted wildly, desperately. "You told me that Maisie—"

"Callie Jackson's a liar," Brandon howled. "Just like Tiff. You've been conned, dude."

"That's enough out of you, Lloyd." The officer towed Brandon to the cruiser.

"It's not true. It can't be true." Jake's hand shot out, capturing Callie's wrist. She winced.

"Tell me." His tortured eyes pleaded. "Tell me Maisie is mine. I'll believe you if you tell me. Please…" His voice broke.

Callie touched his hand, still holding on to her wrist. "Tiff was running from Brandon when she came to the orchard. He wanted her to give up the baby. Even as far gone as Tiff was, she couldn't do that. She wouldn't do that."

He fisted his hands. "I thought Tiffany came to you straight from the base."

Callie gripped his arm. "Tiff was afraid of him. She never wanted him to get his hands on Maisie. Somehow she already knew she was dying. Tiff refused to discuss Maisie's father when I asked. But she put your name on the birth certificate. Maisie looks so much like you. And after knowing you, I couldn't bear for you to be hurt—"

"Maisie's not my..." Jake squeezed his eyes shut. "Why, then, did she put my name on the birth certificate?"

"I think Tiff was trying to protect Maisie from Brandon."

His eyes snapped open. "Why did you ever bother to contact me? Why?"

"Tiff had taken money from Brandon. She used it to get to the farm. She knew he'd come after her one day." Callie took a deep breath. "I think Tiff believed if you were in Maisie's life she'd be safe from him."

"And you...you let me believe..." Jake choked.

"I convinced myself—" She took a ragged breath. "From the moment I met you, I wanted you to be Maisie's father so badly." She gulped. "So badly."

"You were buying his silence to cover Tiffany's lies." Anger radiated off him in waves.

"In every way that really matters, Jake, you are Maisie's father. She loves you. I love—" She threaded her fingers into his. "I was trying to protect you."

He flung off her hand. "You were trying to protect yourself. And he's right about me." He jerked his chin toward the police cruiser. "I trusted you. Fool me once, shame on you. But twice?" He scrubbed his hand over his face. "Tiffany, now you. Shame on me."

Pivoting, he stalked toward the truck.

"Wait, Jake." She caught his shirttail. "It wasn't like that." The fabric ripped in her hand.

He threw open the truck door. "Amber, you better catch another ride to town. I have to pack my gear. Won't take long."

"Please, let me explain. Let's do the paternity test. Be sure." Callie ran to the truck as he slammed the door in her face. "You don't have to leave the orchard, Jake."

"Why drag out the inevitable? When has anything ever turned out the way I hoped?" Through the open window, he glared at her. "I think this pretty much guarantees I have to go, Callie."

She shuddered at the sound of her name between his clenched lips. Like he hated her. And she didn't blame him.

"Jake, if you only knew how much I wanted

Maisie to be yours. How much I wanted everything to be true."

His lips flattened. "What do you know about truth? Got to say, though, I never saw this coming. Not from you."

She could hardly bear the expression in his eyes. The hurt, betrayal. "Jake, please forgive me. I never meant—"

"Forgive you?" His breath frosted the air between them. "I believed you were different. I believed— I hoped that we…" Dropping his head, he cranked the ignition. "You are exactly like Tiffany. Forgiveness is for fools."

Her face covered with her hands, tears ran between her fingers. Callie stepped away as he reversed and made a wide circle in the barren yard. He'd never forgive her. Not for this.

Everything between them was over. She had only herself to blame. She'd lost him forever.

Her heart shattered into a million jagged shards of glass.

Chapter Seventeen

Jake didn't remember driving back to the orchard. The darkening sky. The small white farmhouses along the road. Everything was a blur.

While in the Helmand Province three years ago, he'd received the letter from Tiffany's attorney. Notified that she'd filed for divorce, he'd been so hurt and angry.

But he reeled at the enormity of Callie's betrayal. In one fell swoop, he'd gone from utter happiness to horrific loss. The orchard, Nash and—worst of all—his child.

Parking at the house, he rested his forehead against the steering wheel. Maisie wasn't his child. She was Tiffany's daughter with that jailhouse cretin.

As for Callie? The hurt sliced so deep he could barely draw breath. He hadn't realized a person could feel such emotional pain and their heart still continue to beat. This was what came from trusting people. From lov—

He threw himself out of the truck. A hard life lesson he'd learned early and forgotten the moment he laid eyes on the brown-eyed, tawny-haired farm girl.

Light shone from the front windows, dappling the gray-planked porch. From inside came the low sound of Nash's voice and Maisie's fluted tone. In the years to come, would she ever remember the brief autumn she spent with the man she'd called "my daddy"?

Still unfamiliar with the switchback mountain roads, he couldn't risk leaving tonight. After tomorrow morning, he'd never see Maisie again. He'd never feel her little arms around his neck. He'd lost his baby.

He'd lost everything. A job he loved. A father figure. Callie. Though, considering the secret she'd kept from him, Callie had probably never been his to start with.

Not in the mood for company, he headed for the darkest corner on the wraparound porch. Trust no one. Love no one. Forgive no one?

His conscience smote him, but he stoked the anger brewing inside his heart. Shimmering stars glittered overhead, and he lifted his face to the night sky. Only silence echoed across the valley.

When headlight beams played across the

meadow, signaling Callie's return, he pushed off the railing and went inside.

Nash waited for him at the bottom of the stairs. "I'm sorry, Jake. I didn't know."

She must've texted her dad, giving him a heads-up. It meant a lot to know that Nash hadn't been in on the secret, too.

Jake gripped the newel post. "I can't stay here. Not after this. You know that, right?"

For the first time since Jake had known him, Nash looked every bit of his fifty-plus years. "I understand, son."

Jake had waited a lifetime for someone to call him son, but now... At the age of seven, he'd decided crying was a waste of time. He turned his face to the wall, willing himself not to tear up.

"I want you to know how much I appreciate you letting me stay here, Mr. Jackson, sir, and get to know my—" He blinked rapidly, unable to look at Nash. "Get to know Maisie. I've loved it here."

Nash cleared his throat. "I've loved having you here, Jake."

He allowed himself a swift glance at Nash. "I appreciate everything you taught me about farming. About God." He sucked in a breath. "You gave me the chance to start over."

Nash's eyes pooled. "Jake, I wish—"

"If wishes were apples, you'd be rich, Mr. Jackson, sir."

A crooked smile briefly lightened Nash's countenance.

Jake swallowed. "If you'd allow me to stay one more night, I'll be out of here first light."

"Pop-Pop?" Maisie called from the living room. "My daddy?"

Jake couldn't find enough oxygen to fill his lungs. "I—I can't, sir. Not tonight. Not until I get myself together. I'll say goodbye tomorrow. Tell Maisie I'm…" He rubbed his hand over the spot where his heart used to reside. "Tell her whatever you think best."

Nash pulled Jake into a hug. "I want you to know you are the finest young man I've ever known. I'd hoped…"

Jake stepped away. "I'd hoped, too, sir. But…"

Anguish rolling over him, he placed his hand on the wall to steady himself. If only he could get to the privacy of his room before he completely gave way. "I think it's better if I just go."

This time Nash let him go. And Jake made his escape. To mourn his losses. And weep for what would never be.

Staring at the ceiling, Jake didn't sleep that night. Why did nothing good ever last for him?

Lying there, he tried to imagine a future without his baby girl. A future away from the awe-inspiring presence of the mountains. A future without the woman he loved. Callie—perhaps the only woman he'd ever truly loved. Probably the only woman he would ever love.

He buried his face in the mattress. He'd learned his lesson good this time. No more risking his heart. Her betrayal had reopened a scabbed-over wound that had never completely healed.

Jake felt bereft of everything and everyone that for a brief time had made his life actually worth living. Emptiness consumed him.

The childhood tape with his father's voice played in his head. He'd been right about Jake. This nothingness was exactly what he deserved. He was worthless. Not worth loving.

But that was not what the pastor had said. Nor Nash and Callie.

He punched the pillow under his head. So what was the truth? What was the lie?

With sleep impossible, he rose at the first pink streaks of light. Placing his duffel in the truck, he retrieved Callie's camera to return to her and ventured out to the orchard in the quiet of dawn. The dew dampening his brown boots, he walked among the apple trees.

Finally slipping into the house, he found Callie alone in the kitchen. He laid the camera on the countertop. "This is yours."

"Oh, Jake..."

"Where's your father?"

"Dad's in the barn. I don't think he could face any more farewells." The sprinkle of freckles stark against her ashen face, she looked as bad as he felt. "Were you going to leave without saying goodbye?"

"My daddy!" Erupting out of the hallway, a tiny dynamo of blond energy flung herself at him. Maisie raised her arms.

He hesitated, but he could no more resist those smiling blueberry eyes of hers than he could will his body not to take its next breath.

Jake lifted her into his arms. "What have you told her?"

"I didn't know what to say…"

He hated how the sound of her voice made his pulse jackhammer.

"I hoped this morning that you…" Callie's brown eyes were red rimmed. "I'm so sorry, Jake," she whispered.

He steeled himself for the most painful goodbye of all. "Maisie, Daddy has to go—" He swallowed. "I mean *I've* got to go."

"'Kay, my daddy. Mowow?"

He touched his forehead to hers. "I don't know about tomorrow, baby. But I want you to be a good girl for Pop-Pop and Callie."

Maisie hung on to him, her arms around his neck. "Me big gull, my daddy."

Jake sank onto the sofa. "Yes, you are," he choked. "A very big girl that I am so proud of."

He needed to leave before he lost what little remnant of pride he had left.

"Sing Mah-mah-may-zee song, my daddy."

From Maisie's upturned face, his gaze flitted to Callie.

Her features crumpled. She whirled around to the kitchen island, unable to hold in her tears.

But at least now she wasn't watching him pour out his heart to the daughter never meant to be his.

Cradling Maisie to his chest, he gathered his courage and one final time inhaled her little-girl fresh-from-the-tub sweetness.

"My daddy…" Maisie prompted. "Sing. Me."

The ache in his chest became a stabbing throb.

"'M-M-M-Maisie, beautiful Maisie…'"

Her silky curls brushing his jaw, she tucked her head in the curve of his shoulder.

"'You're the only g-g-g-girl that I adore…'" His voice scratched low in his throat.

She made a soft sighing sound like a little mewling kitten.

"'When the m-m-m-moon shines over the cowshed…'"

Nestling deeper into his embrace, she pressed her cheek against the V of exposed skin above the collar of his flannel shirt.

His heart pounded, momentarily deafening him. How could he leave her? How—

"My daddy." Maisie stirred.

"'I'll be waiting at the k-k-k-kitchen door…'" His voice broke.

There was a brief silence except for the ticking of the mantel clock and the stricken sound of Callie's muffled sobs.

Sitting up in his lap, Maisie placed her small, warm palms against his cheeks, tugging him closer. "I wuv you, my daddy."

He cupped her face in his hand. "And I will love you always, my Maisie." With his thumb, he stroked the dimple in her chin.

Abruptly rising, he staggered to his feet.

Monkey legs wrapped tightly around his torso, Maisie clung to his neck. "Take her, Callie," he grunted.

Callie closed the distance between them. "Please don't go, Jake." She reached out to him, but dropped her hand. "I love you."

Her words were like a kick in the gut. After what she'd done and not done? Now she was telling him that she loved him? He stared at her, incredulous.

Anger surged inside him, tying his stomach into knots. "That would make one of us, then," he growled.

Mouth trembling, she looked as if he'd struck her.

Something stronger than his anger punched him square in the chest. He shouldn't have said that. It wasn't true. He did love her.

It was the pain that made him lash out at her,

wanting her to hurt as much as she'd hurt him. But he didn't really want to hurt her.

After he left, he hoped—prayed—one day a good man would make a home with Callie and the child Jake loved more than anyone on earth. Because he loved them, he wanted them to be happy.

Even if happy meant being happy without him.

One arm draped around Jake, Maisie wrapped her other arm around Callie, pulling the three of them closer. A human bridge, joining them together as if they were a real family.

"Where…" Callie moistened her lips. "Where will you go?" she whispered.

Lips he would never kiss again. But the memory of their kiss sizzled his brain.

He scoured his face with his hand. "Perhaps Houston."

She put her hand over her mouth.

"I'll send money."

She shook her head.

He held up his hand. "Doesn't matter what DNA she's got in her veins. I intend to provide for her even though after today, I won't ever see her again."

Callie's eyes widened. "Jake, you can't do that to her. You can't walk away like your parents walked away from—"

"It's not the same."

"It is the same." Callie's nostrils flared. "She won't understand."

"Maisie will forget me." His mouth tightened. "Remember Tiffany? I'm extremely forgettable."

"Not to me," Callie rasped. "Maisie loves you. She belongs with you. You belong with each other."

He stared at her. "What are you saying?"

"I could think of nothing else all night." Tears ran down Callie's cheeks. "I'm saying I can't let you leave without Maisie. She needs to go with you."

He stiffened. "What about her biological father?"

"Your name is on her birth certificate." The look in Callie's dark eyes was unwavering. "Besides, Brandon doesn't want her, Jake. He never did."

Jake grimaced. "That doesn't change the fact that Maisie needs you, Callie. You are her true mother."

Her gaze softened, flickering to Maisie. "I think right now she needs you more." Her eyes locked with his. "I think right now you need her more. I can't allow you to lose each other again, Jake."

"But Texas…the job… My future is uncertain."

"You'll make it work. I trust you to see to her best interests." Pulling away from Maisie's tight hold, Callie dashed the tears from her eyes. "Do you want Maisie in your life, Jake? Because if you do, she's yours. She's always been yours."

"I want her." He hugged Maisie close. "I've always wanted her."

You, too. But he didn't say that. Despite everything, he still wanted Callie. More fool he.

That was where he went wrong. He'd talked himself into believing he could have more. That the dream of his heart would come true. That he'd found a home with Callie.

But despite Maisie leaving with him, the little girl's home should always include Callie.

He shifted Maisie higher in his arms. "I think it would be in her best interests for us to share custody."

The gratitude on her face nearly felled him. "Thank you, Jake." She clasped her hands under her chin. "Dad and I can visit you wherever you are or Maisie can visit us here."

Because of Maisie, he and Callie would be forever tied. But that didn't disturb him as much as his anger said it should.

He hunched his shoulders. "Whatever you think."

"I think for the time being, Maisie belongs with you." She put her hand to her throat. "If you'll give me a few minutes—twenty tops—I'll pack the essentials for Maisie. When you get settled, we can ship the rest."

Maisie stretched out her hand. "BooWoo?"

She couldn't possibly understand they were deciding her future. Or that it would be a very long time before she saw Callie, Nash and the orchard again.

Callie's eyes were bleak—she understood enough for the both of them. "Will you wait, Jake?"

His Adam's apple bobbed. "I'll wait."

Callie buzzed around the farmhouse, perhaps afraid if she stopped for a second, she wouldn't be able to go through with it.

But she had the truck loaded in nineteen minutes flat. When Nash came inside, Callie told him about her decision.

Jake felt sure he'd pitch a fit, but he didn't. Instead, he filled Maisie's sippy cup with her favorite, 'appy juice. Nash placed a tender, gentle kiss on Maisie's cheek.

After strapping Maisie into Jake's truck, Callie handed BooWoo over the seat to Maisie. At the expression on her face, he thought she might lose it. But neither of them wanted to break down in front of Maisie.

Pressing a kiss onto Maisie's furrowed forehead, Callie took a quick, indrawn breath. Maybe, as he'd done earlier, she was trying to memorize Maisie's scent, the feel of the child in her arms.

Stepping away, Callie closed the cab door. Looking over the roof of the cab at the torment in her eyes, his legs suddenly wouldn't support him. He couldn't do this to her.

"Callie…"

She shook her head. "Go. Now. Please, Jake. Before—" Clamping her lips together, she fled to the porch and her father.

Behind the wheel, he cranked the engine. Nausea licked at his belly. This wasn't the way he'd wanted things to play out.

Leaning heavily against the railing, Nash's face was a study in grief. Jake had never wanted to hurt either of them.

This was killing Callie. This was killing him. But they'd hurt each other too much. And now it was too late.

"Bwye, Cawee." Angling in the car seat, Maisie waved from the rear windshield. "Bwye."

Pulling away from the farmhouse, he glanced in the rearview mirror as Callie sank onto the step. Shoulders shaking, she buried her face in her hands. And that was the last thing he saw before the truck sped over the rise.

Unlike that first day, today he didn't stop. He didn't turn the truck around. Gritting his teeth, he set his face forward.

But his heart was broken.

Chapter Eighteen

Passing the shuttered Apple House, Jake left the long gravel-covered driveway and turned onto the main road. Behind him, strapped into her pink car seat, Maisie whispered to BooWoo in little-girl speak.

Reaching Truelove, he carried Maisie into the police station. He answered a few questions about the incident last night and filled out the required paperwork with the officer in charge. Because of Nash's standing in the community, it didn't take long. Like the good man he was, Nash had already called his friend this morning to vouch for Jake.

Jake and Maisie returned to the truck. Leaving Truelove behind them, he headed toward the highway. Maybe when they got to Asheville, he'd stop and get Maisie a snack.

Up with the chickens, his early-bird little farm girl had eaten before he'd made it downstairs.

Sick to his stomach, he hadn't felt much like eating. Still didn't.

"'Appy?"

His gaze flicked to the mirror.

Maisie pointed at the rows of apple orchards on both sides of the road. He remembered the first time he'd driven this highway. Late summer rolled hay bales had dotted the grassy meadows. Now the fields lay fallow and bare, ready for winter.

The image of Callie's photo rose in his mind. A picture of the barn and orchard covered in a blanket of snow. And in the backdrop, the ever-present solace of snow-daubed mountains.

He didn't know where winter would find him and Maisie, but he was pretty sure there'd be no comfort for him there. Or anywhere.

Gripping the wheel, he veered at the fork. He let out a breath, uncurling one hand. He flexed his fingers and tried to relax. Tried to recapture an elusive peace. The peace he'd first encountered at the mountain chapel.

They climbed out of the valley. As the elevation rose, he worked his jaw to pop his eardrums. The towering peaks of the evergreen-studded Blue Ridge flashed by on both sides of the embankment.

He slowed. Coming to a dead end, he allowed the truck to roll until the pavement stopped. He shook his head.

Unbelievable. How had he wound up on the same deserted country road as that first day when he'd been on the way to meet his daughter? Why did he keep ending up here?

He hadn't known much then. He didn't know much now. But he did know when he was in the middle of nowhere, lost and going nowhere fast. Was God trying to tell him something?

Maisie kicked the back of his seat with her foot. "Out, my daddy. Out."

Sighing, he put the truck in Park and let the engine idle. Undoing his seat belt, he put his knee into the cushion, leaning over to unbuckle Maisie.

"Come here, big girl."

He helped her clamber into the front with him. Standing on the upholstery, she planted a kiss on his scruffy jaw. He smiled.

She plopped beside him on the seat. Bouncing a little, she cut her eyes at him, a tiny gleam in their clear blue depths.

He had to fight not to smile. "No more monkeys, Maisie."

Tilting her head, she fluttered her lashes at him and he laughed. The little heartbreaker was working him. He'd have his hands full with this one in about a dozen years.

Sorrow pummeled him. He'd hoped to raise her with Callie.

But single parent though he was, he'd ensure

love encompassed every second of Maisie's life. His love for her would be as constant as the air she breathed.

Scooting over to the glove compartment, Maisie crawled off the seat. Jiggling the handle, her eyebrow arched. "My daddy?"

On a good day, he could refuse Maisie nothing. And this was far from a good day.

He switched off the ignition. "Let me look first." To make sure the contents didn't pose a hazard to a curious two-year-old. "What do we have here, Maisie?"

Opening the compartment, he rummaged, finding extra napkins from a fast-food drive-through. He set aside the owner's manual. A flashlight... A North Carolina map—he was old-school that way. And...the bunch of mail from the Fayetteville post office. He'd forgotten about that.

He pocketed a pressure gauge. Everything else was junk. "Have at it, Maze."

Jake rolled his window down an inch so their breath didn't fog the windshield. A little nippy for early November, but not too bad.

He leaned against the headrest, letting her play for a few minutes. He wasn't in a hurry. Until he contacted his buddy, he had no place to be.

Birdsong floated through the air. A bright red flash caught his eye as a cardinal landed on a nearby branch. His thoughts wandered.

He could hardly believe the sacrifice Callie had made in sending Maisie with him. His heart had been breaking at the prospect of missing his little girl.

Jake ran his hand over his head. He couldn't imagine how rough it must be for Callie. He'd expected to drive away alone, but how alone must she feel now?

Pushing the button, Maisie discovered how to power on the flashlight. She laughed. Off and on. On and off. Spotlighting the dashboard. Shining the light on the floor mat.

Jake recalled the hopelessness he'd felt that first day as he deposited her in Callie's arms. Walking away, believing he'd never see his child again.

Holding the flashlight under her chin, Maisie turned the light on herself. She smiled at him. He smiled back.

Look at how far he and Maisie had come. Like two pages glued together, unable to be separated without damaging them both. But without Callie, he wasn't sure he'd ever feel truly whole again.

That first day when he'd behaved so badly, Callie had been gracious. Forgiving him. Offering him a second chance with Maisie. An opportunity to prove himself. To win their trust.

So why couldn't he do the same and return the favor to her? Was facing a future without

Callie in his life worth hanging on to the anger and bitterness?

Laying the flashlight aside, Maisie moved on to further explorations. She shuffled through the junk mail, and several envelopes fell between her feet.

Quickly losing interest, she dropped the rest and climbed onto the seat again. She curled against his side. Warmth and tenderness flooded him.

He loved Maisie so much. He placed his arm around her shoulders, snuggling her against him. Callie loved her so much.

When he stopped fuming, he could acknowledge that in keeping Tiffany's secret, she hadn't intended to hurt him. She'd been protecting Maisie. Trying to protect him, too.

"BooWoo, my daddy..." Maisie's eyes drooped.

He kissed her forehead. "BooWoo needs a nap."

Mouth puckered, eyes closed, she nodded. He wasn't the only one exhausted from an overly full weekend at the festival. The past few days had been turbulent, as well. She was off her routine.

"Let's put you back with BooWoo, baby."

"'Kay, my daddy."

Half-asleep, she didn't protest as he strapped her into the car seat. BooWoo cuddled tight to her chest, her breaths became slow and even.

Jake reckoned he'd never get his fill of watching Maisie. The sheer marvel of her existence. The exquisite joy of being a part of her life.

And as he watched her sleep, his pulse settled. The anger seeped from him. How far would *he* have gone for love? As far as Callie?

He had his answer in the gentle rise and fall of Maisie's chest. He would go to any lengths to protect the child he loved as his own. He pressed his forehead against the wheel.

I forgave Tiffany. I really did, God. But after what Callie did to me? How can I forgive her?

Yet, how could he not? Jake sucked in a breath. Despite a lifetime of mistakes, God had forgiven him.

Because that was what a good, loving father did. He'd learned that from Nash Jackson. When you loved someone, you forgave them.

The real question he needed to ask himself was which did he love more. The anger that kept him, Maisie and Callie forever apart? Or forgiveness, which opened a future for him to make a real family for Maisie with Callie?

His bitterness kept him tied to a past he'd do better to put behind him. Why would he want to live bound to misery when he could have so much more with Callie?

Did he love Callie? His breath came in rapid spurts. Yes, he loved her more than he'd ever believed possible. Was he willing to throw away what he felt for Callie and what they could be to each other because of pride? No, his heart roared within him, he wasn't.

God, I love her so much. Forgive me for lashing out in anger instead of letting her explain. For running away when I should have forgiven her and stayed to work things out.

With his child sleeping in the back seat, the longer he sat there, the more at peace he felt. A burden he was never meant to carry had lifted from his shoulders. He found himself bestowing forgiveness on everyone who'd ever hurt him—even his father, though it wasn't easy.

It was then he knew he was ready, with God's help, to be the man he was meant to be. The father he should be. The husband he yet hoped to become.

He glanced at his sleeping child, BooWoo cuddled under her chin. What kind of life could he make for himself and Maisie if their hearts had lost their home?

What did home look like for them? But in his heart, he already knew.

Home looked like a white farmhouse on a knoll overlooking an apple orchard. Home looked like a mountainside chapel and a small Blue Ridge town called Truelove. But most of all, home looked like Callie Jackson.

Maybe he'd already damaged beyond repair his relationship with her. Or would she give him a second chance to make things right? He squared his shoulders. Only one way to find out.

Blowing out a breath, he started the engine. Putting the truck in gear, he cranked the wheel hard and headed out of the dead-end road. Back the way he'd come.

Help her to forgive me, Father. He swallowed. *Help her to still want me in her life. Help her to still love me.*

But no matter what, he and Maisie were going home.

They were gone.

Callie didn't know how she was going to go on without them. Though equally devastated, her dad had agreed that Maisie belonged with Jake. And so, at last, she'd done the right thing.

The secret had cost her everything.

Leaning against the porch railing, she moaned. Why did the right thing always have to hurt so much? Her father had wandered off into the orchard. Beneath the crisp, tangy scent of the apples, he would pray and find his consolation.

Without Jake and Maisie, there was no place of consolation for Callie. Only empty arms and an aching heart awaited her. Overwhelmed with the pain of loss, she went inside the house and stumbled up the staircase.

She hesitated outside Jake's bedroom. She ought to strip the bed and wash the sheets. The room was a mere hollowed-out echo of his presence. As hollowed out as her heart felt.

Going inside she noticed that the closet door stood slightly ajar. Curious, she found one of Jake's shirts crumpled in a puddle in the far corner. It was the shirt he'd worn yesterday. The one with the ripped shirttail. Needing to touch something of his, she plucked it off the floor and wandered into Maisie's room.

Kicking off her flats, she lay on the big-girl bed and pressed her cheek against Maisie's small pillow. Bringing Jake's chambray shirt to her nostrils, she inhaled the clean, spicy scent of him. As close as she'd ever get to him again. She'd lost him forever.

Callie squeezed her eyes tight against the treacherous trickle of tears. *I love you. I love you. I love you.* But Jake didn't love her. Sobs shaking her body, she buried her face in his shirt.

She awoke with a start, her heart pounding. Exhausted from a sleepless night and the life-altering events of the morning, she must have cried herself to sleep.

How long had she been asleep? Rays of mid-morning light filtered through the lacy pink curtains. A few hours? Her gaze fell to the storybook lying on Maisie's little table. *Sleeping Beauty.*

A flicker of hope ignited within her heart.

Please, God, let the past twenty-four hours have been a horrible dream.

Hugging Jake's shirt, she sat up. And reality came crashing back. No dream.

She inched to the edge of the mattress, her foot feeling for her flats somewhere on the rug. Shoes on, she dragged herself off the bed. Had a school group been scheduled to tour the orchard today? If so, Dad would be going crazy.

Her face felt gritty from the salt residue of her tears. With the first wave of intense grief past, numbness blanketed her emotions. Would the numbed feeling last forever?

But happy or sad, farm life went on, as did the chores waiting to be done. She slipped Jake's shirt over her blouse. Rolling the sleeves to her elbows, she headed downstairs.

Maybe if she worked herself into exhaustion, by nightfall she'd be able to sleep instead of staring at the ceiling yearning for Maisie and Jake.

She found her dad in the barn. His eyes crinkled with concern. She ran a hand through her hair. "I should have been out here helping you this morning. I'm sorry."

"Don't be sorry. Are you okay?"

"No…" She gave a shuddery breath. "But when the going gets tough, farm girls get going."

Her dad enfolded her in a tight hug. "You don't have to hide your feelings from me, Callie Girl. I'm missing them right alongside you."

She stepped back, wiping her cheeks. "No tour group this morning?"

Her father shook his head. "Only school morning this entire season without a group. I guess the good Lord knew we'd need this morning to ourselves."

A cloud of dust signaled the arrival of a visitor turning in off the road. The last of the leaf peepers wandering off the Blue Ridge Parkway. The trees at the top of the ridge had lost their leaves. The vibrant reds and yellows of the leaves in the valley had dulled. Autumn, like her dreams, was over.

"GeorgeAnne and the matchmakers are manning the store. I'll make sure they're doing okay. You should take some time for yourself today."

She made a face. "I've spent the whole morning by myself."

"Take the shortcut through the meadow." He nudged his chin toward the orchard. "Walk among the trees for a few minutes. Talk to the Lord."

She looked at him. "I have the best father in the world."

Her dad laughed. "I don't know about that, but the best heavenly Father for sure."

She meandered through the meadow. Trailing her hand along the tops of the goldenrod and purple asters, she became aware of the silhouette of a man standing near the edge of the meadow.

Customers didn't usually venture beyond the Apple House. Of all days… Where was her dad?

Blinded by the angle of the sun, she threw up her hand to shade her eyes. "Are you here to buy apples?" she called, gesturing toward the road. "You've driven right past the Apple House." She hurried, picking her way through the tall grass. "It's the building next to—"

"Callie."

She froze. Jake?

It couldn't be him. He and Maisie were on their way to Texas. Yet, backlit by the sun, it looked like Jake's strong, muscled frame. Or just wishful thinking?

The man strode toward her. "Callie."

Her heart hitched. It *was* Jake. Her thoughts in a jumble, she peered around him. "Where's Maisie?"

"Maisie's with Pop-Pop."

With Jake blocking the sun, she spotted the glint of his truck in the driveway.

Trembling, she wrapped Jake's shirt around herself. "Is—is something wrong?"

"I forgot to tell you something. And I also need to ask you to forgive me."

She bit her lip. "You haven't done anything wrong."

He stuck his hands in his jeans. "I know you never meant to hurt me. But I let the knee-jerk reactions of a lifetime drown out what my heart was telling me to be true."

"Jake, you don't have anything to apologize for."

"Yes, I do." A muscle ticked in his jaw. "I hope you'll forgive me for not believing you."

"Of course I forgive you, Jake. I love you." Her mouth quivered. "I know I've ruined everything, but somehow do you think you could find it in your heart to forgive me?"

"I forgive you, Callie."

"Thank you, Jake."

Callie laced her hands together lest she give in to the temptation to touch him. The need to feel his arms around her was like a physical ache, but because of her actions, she'd forfeited any future with him.

She heaved a sigh. "I should give Maisie another hug before you head out again." But she wasn't sure her heart could stand another goodbye. With him, either.

He cocked his head. "Is that what you want? For me and Maisie to leave?"

"I never wanted…" She blinked. "But I thought—"

"You haven't asked me what I forgot to tell you, Callie."

She lowered her gaze. "Your forgiveness means the world to me, Jake."

"That's not everything I wanted to say to you,

Callie. I couldn't get out of the county before I realized that leaving here was nothing but a dead-end road to nowhere."

She was almost afraid to hope, to imagine he'd changed his mind about leaving. "If you stay in Truelove with Maisie, Dad and I will help you find just the right place to—"

He shook his head. "I don't think that arrangement would suit me, Callie. Anyway, there's the matchmakers to consider."

Callie's heart sank. She'd misunderstood his intentions about staying. "Oh."

"What I mean is, the matchmakers were right. Pretty near right about everything. Go figure."

"Jake, I—"

"Maisie isn't the only one I found impossible to leave." He captured her hand. "I can't leave you, Callie. I love you."

He loved her? But was love enough to overcome what she'd done?

Jake took a ragged breath. "I think I've loved you since the first evening when you walked in the meadow with Maisie."

Tears pricked her eyelids. "But I destroyed your trust in me, Jake."

"You're the one who told me that trust can be rebuilt." He pulled her closer. "You gave me a second chance with Maisie. I want a second chance with you. A second chance to love you. If you'll have me, Callie."

His hands circled her waist. Fingers splayed against his chest, she rested her cheek upon the soft fabric of his shirt. Callie closed her eyes, feeling the thrumming vibration of his heartbeat.

Was this really happening? Jake loved her? After everything she had done?

He tightened his grip, bending his head. His lips brushed her ear. "Will you have me, Callie?" he whispered, his voice husky and low. "I promise, if you'll give me another chance to show you how much I love you, I won't ever leave you again."

She lifted her face to him. "That's a promise I'm going to hold you to, soldier."

His eyes—as blue as a Carolina sky—crinkled at the corners. "That's a yes, then?"

"Most definitely a yes."

His arms tightened. If she had only one moment to live forever, she'd want it to be this moment. Finally, when he loosened his hold, she stepped back, but not far. She never wanted to be far from his embrace again.

"Shall we go tell Dad and Maisie the good news?"

"First…" Running his hand down her arm, he gave her that lovely, lopsided smile of his. "Does it look like rain to you, farm girl?"

Lips twitching, she craned her neck, peering at the not-a-cloud sky over the mountain ridge. "Why, yes, Jake McAbee, I think you're right."

He smiled. "Time to collect on that rain check you promised."

She tucked her tongue into her cheek. "And I guess that means you'll be wanting a kiss?"

"One. Or two." He swung her around. "Or three."

"So what are you waiting for, then?" Lifting her mouth to his, she slipped her arms around his neck. "Kiss me, Jake."

And he did.

Epilogue

Prisms of color splashed the interior of his truck. Jake smiled.

For what had to be the tenth time since they'd left Truelove, Callie pivoted her hand this way and that, admiring the ring he just purchased. Catching the light, her brand-new engagement ring sparkled on her finger.

Behind them in her car seat, Maisie sang one of her little-girl songs to BooWoo. A song that went something like "Bah-bah-bah-BooWoo, beautiful BooWoo…"

Her brown eyes dancing, Callie's gaze darted to him. Lips curving, Jake had never been happier in his life.

In Truelove, he'd found everything he'd ever wanted and more. More than he'd ever imagined possible for someone like him. Correction, a child of God like him. It would take a while to undo the false thought patterns of a lifetime.

He'd decided against going through with the paternity test. He'd rather live with uncertainty than with a painful truth. He'd love Maisie either way. And if he could love Maisie like that, how much more must God's love for him be? Fathomless.

Pulling in front of the farmhouse, he cut the engine. He took a moment and contemplated the mountain vista in the distance. The tidy put-to-bed-for-winter appearance of the orchard. It was good to be still. To soak in the blessings of the day.

With Jake's hands on the steering wheel, Callie wrapped her arm around his. "I'm not ready to go in yet, either."

"Out, my daddy!" Maisie kicked the seat. "Out."

Jake rolled his eyes.

"Or not." Callie laughed. "The queen bee has spoken."

Sliding out of his seat belt, he twisted around to unbuckle Maisie. "Not every bride takes a two-year-old along to pick out her engagement ring. Did you mind?"

Her shoulder brushed his as Callie angled to help him. "Why would I mind? It was Maisie who brought me the love of my life."

Jake's heart slammed against his rib cage. The

love shining from Callie's face was like nothing he'd ever known before. Filling him with hope for tomorrow's bright possibilities. And a deep humility for God's goodness.

He stopped fiddling with the buckles long enough to plant a kiss on the slender curve of Callie's neck. He smacked his lips. "Apples and cinnamon. My favorite."

Smiling, she blushed.

"Out!" Maisie bucked. "Mommy! My daddy!"

Callie released the last clasp. "Just a minute, silly girl."

But he sensed Callie's deep pleasure. A recent, unprompted development, Maisie had taken to calling her *Mommy.*

Maisie opened her arms.

Jake lifted her out and over the top of the seat. "I want the wedding to be everything you dreamed, Callie." He settled Maisie between them.

Callie smoothed a golden curl off Maisie's forehead. "It will be. It is." She gave him a shy glance. "As long as we're together."

Maisie crawled over Callie, hopping off the seat to the floor.

He tugged Callie closer. "Together, forever."

With a happy sigh, she snuggled underneath his arm.

He nuzzled her hair with his cheek. "You sure I have to wait till Thanksgiving to marry you?"

"As it is, Miss GeorgeAnne is having a fit, Jake. We've only given the matchmakers two weeks to prepare." But Callie's smile belied her words.

He huffed. "Sure as they were, you'd have thought they would've had everything ready, minus the date on the invitations."

She elbowed him. "Got to give 'em credit. They took one look at you and knew a good thing when they saw it."

He kissed her cheek. "So did I."

"Do you mind, Jake?" She bit her lip. "The flowers. The hoopla?"

Taking her hand, he threaded his fingers in hers. "I don't mind. I want the world to know how much I love Callie Rose Jackson."

She quirked her eyebrow. "Soon to be Callie Jackson McAbee."

"Not soon enough for me."

Bringing her hand to his mouth, he kissed the ring on her finger. "It's a first for me, too. A five-minute ceremony with the justice of the peace isn't the same." His gaze locked on to hers. "This is the way it ought to be. It's new for me. Beautiful. You know that, right? Everything I feel for you, it's so much more than I ever—"

"I know, Jake." She took his face in her hands. "The past brought us to each other. There are no secrets between us. I understand about Tiff. It's okay."

Jake searched her face. He'd spend his life making sure she never felt uncertain about her place in his heart. "I love you so much, Callie."

Her smile stole his breath. "I love you, too. The bestest." Letting go of him, she leaned over and kissed Maisie's head. "The mostest. The biggest."

Digging under the seat, Maisie didn't look up.

"Besides..." Callie gave him a sideways look. "It's only two weeks. Then I'll have you all to myself for seven days."

There was a sound of paper ripping.

She glanced over to the floorboard. "Maisie? What have you got there, sweetie?"

Maisie rose, a torn envelope in her small hand.

Jake drummed his fingers on the wheel. "She was playing with that last week. I should have cleaned it up, but..." He rolled his tongue in his cheek. "Been a little preoccupied."

Her lips twitching, Callie took the crumpled envelope from Maisie. She examined the postmark and frowned. "What in the world? It's dated almost three years ago. Postmarked Fayetteville."

"On my last trip to the base, I emptied out the post office box Tiffany set up." He shrugged. "Just junk."

"It doesn't look like junk mail to me, Jake." Removing the key from the ignition, Callie slit open the envelope. She unfolded the paper inside. "This looks impor—" She gasped.

He straightened. "What?"

Tears swam in her eyes.

"Callie?"

"Oh, Jake." She clasped the paper to her chest. "It's true. I prayed… I knew it had to be true."

"What's true?"

She thrust the paper at him. "It's a copy of a lab report. From an obstetrician's office." Her face transformed. "In Fayetteville, Jake. Fayetteville."

His hand shook as he took the paper from her.

Callie's eyes glistened. "The timing. Everything fits."

Almost afraid to read it, he scanned the document. "A prenatal office visit." He looked at Callie. "Maisie?" he whispered.

Callie took both his hands in hers. "She's your daughter, Jake."

"She's mine…" He cut his gaze to Maisie, happily playing in the foot of the truck with more unopened mail. His vision blurred. "She's really mine." Wonderment filled his voice.

"For once, Tiff told the truth. She put your name on the birth certificate because you are Maisie's father. She *was* already pregnant when she went to Atlanta."

"Will I ever know why she left in the first place?"

Callie shook her head. "Tiff did inexplicable

things. But I think she realized she'd made a mistake. I just don't get why she came here instead of trying to fix things with you."

"A mistake she didn't know how to fix." He raked his hand over his face. "Actually, I get that part. Because of our childhoods… That's the thing Tiffany and I understood about each other."

Callie's features clouded.

He squeezed Callie's hand. "Until I met you, I didn't believe anyone would ever forgive my mistakes and give me a second chance." He gulped. "But no matter what she'd done, I would have taken her back. If only for Maisie's sake."

Callie cupped his cheek in her palm. "I know that about you, Jake McAbee. Yours is the most loving, forgiving heart I've ever known."

But Tiffany hadn't known it. He felt a tremendous sadness for the pain she'd gone through. Alone by choice. The suffering she'd endured.

"I misunderstood," Callie mused. "She didn't fear Brandon because he was Maisie's father."

Jake nodded. "She was afraid of him because she'd taken his money."

"Because she finally found the courage to walk away from the obsessive hold he had over her." Callie knotted her hands. "She feared he'd take his revenge on Maisie."

"If he couldn't have Tiffany, nobody would?"

"During her final days, Tiff talked about you a lot, Jake. She said she never wanted you to know the truth. And that she was sorry. I thought she meant she never wanted you to know you weren't Maisie's father. That she was sorry you weren't Maisie's father."

Jake's eyes drooped.

Callie hugged his arm. "But now I think she meant she didn't want to hurt you with the truth about her relationship with Brandon. And she was sorry for betraying you. I know that doesn't excuse what she did, but I hope it helps a little."

"It does." He took a cleansing breath. "I made mistakes, too. I didn't love her the way she needed to be loved. Until I met you and God, I didn't understand what love should look like."

"The only one who could love Tiff the way she needed to be loved—who can love any of us the way we need—is God." Callie bit her lip. "At the end of her life, I think Tiff finally discovered Him for herself. I pray so."

Jake sighed. "I don't understand why life turned out the way it did for Tiffany."

"There are things I believe we're not meant to truly understand this side of Heaven. But I believe He can bring beauty even out of such incredible brokenness."

Jake turned his mouth into her palm. "And He has."

"My daddy." Maisie crawled over Callie. "'Appy juice."

Opening the truck door, he eased out. Maisie raised her arms to him. He held her close.

When Callie stepped out, he opened his embrace. His girls, right where they belonged, next to his heart. And Jake, where he belonged, next to theirs.

Nash came out onto the porch.

"Let's go tell Dad." Callie gave him a quick kiss on the cleft in his chin. "He'll be so glad to hear the news." Together, they went to greet him.

Jake had arrived with nothing. Now he had a family. A beautiful bride. A wonderful daughter. Nash.

Thank You, God.

Jake had come home. Not just to Truelove or Apple Valley Farm. He'd found the love of a good, good Father.

And the true home for which they'd all been made.

* * * * *

Dear Reader,

Welcome to Truelove, North Carolina—Where True Love Awaits. This new romantic series is set in the breathtakingly lovely Blue Ridge Mountains of North Carolina.

Though the course of true love doesn't always run smooth, never fear. The Truelove matchmakers are there to make sure everyone finds their true happily-ever-after.

The heart of this story is about a man searching for someplace to belong. He's seeking love and purpose. He's searching for home. This story is also about trusting God. With the good. With the bad. With everything.

Home. What images does that word create in your mind? For some, the memories are good. For others, memories of home are extremely painful.

But I believe the longing for home is at the core of who we are as humans.

As Jake discovers at Apple Valley Farm, no matter how tragic the past or present, God has a place of belonging for each of us. And I believe no matter where you've been, no matter where you are right now, no matter what you've done— that God can take what is broken and make it into something beautiful. In fact, I think He delights in bringing beauty out of brokenness.

Why did I write this story? Because it is my prayer that *no matter where you've been, no matter where you are right now, no matter what you've done*—that you will ultimately find in Him your home. The happily-ever-after for which you were truly made.

I hope you have enjoyed taking this journey with Callie, Jake and Maisie. I would love to hear from you. You may email me at lisa@lisacarter-author.com or visit www.lisacarterauthor.com.

In His Love,
Lisa Carter

Get 4 FREE REWARDS!

We'll send you 2 FREE Books
plus 2 FREE Mystery Gifts.

Love Inspired® Suspense books feature Christian characters facing challenges to their faith... and lives.

FREE Value Over $20

Get 4 FREE REWARDS!

We'll send you 2 FREE Books <u>plus</u> 2 FREE Mystery Gifts.

Harlequin® Heartwarming™ Larger-Print books feature traditional values of home, family, community and—most of all—love.

FREE Value Over **$20**

YES! Please send me 2 FREE Harlequin® Heartwarming™ Larger-Print novels and my 2 FREE mystery gifts (gifts worth about $10 retail). After receiving them, if I don't wish to receive any more books, I can return the shipping statement marked "cancel." If I don't cancel, I will receive 4 brand-new larger-print novels every month and be billed just $5.49 per book in the U.S. or $6.24 per book in Canada. That's a savings of at least 19% off the cover price. It's quite a bargain! Shipping and handling is just 50¢ per book in the U.S. and 75¢ per book in Canada.* I understand that accepting the 2 free books and gifts places me under no obligation to buy anything. I can always return a shipment and cancel at any time. The free books and gifts are mine to keep no matter what I decide.

161/361 IDN GMY3

Name (please print)

Address   Apt. #

City   State/Province   Zip/Postal Code

Mail to the **Reader Service:**
IN U.S.A.: P.O. Box 1341, Buffalo, NY 14240-8531
IN CANADA: P.O. Box 603, Fort Erie, Ontario L2A 5X3

Want to try 2 free books from another series! Call 1-800-873-8635 or visit www.ReaderService.com.

MUST ♥ DOGS COLLECTION

SAVE 30% AND GET A FREE GIFT!

Finding true love can be "ruff"— but not when adorable dogs help to play matchmaker in these inspiring romantic "tails."

YES! Please send me the first shipment of four books from the **Must ♥ Dogs Collection**. If I don't cancel, I will continue to receive four books a month for two additional months, and I will be billed at the same discount price of $18.20 U.S./$20.30 CAN., plus $1.99 for shipping and handling.* That's a 30% discount off the cover prices! Plus, I'll receive a FREE adorable, hand-painted dog figurine in every shipment (approx. retail value of $4.99)! I am under no obligation to purchase anything and I may cancel at any time by marking "cancel" on the shipping statement and returning the shipment. I may keep the FREE books no matter what I decide.

☐ 256 HCN 4331　　　　☐ 456 HCN 4331

Name (please print)

Address　　　　　　　　　　　　　　　　　　　　　　　Apt. #

City　　　　　　　　　State/Province　　　　　　　　Zip/Postal Code

> Mail to the **Reader Service:**
> **IN U.S.A.:** P.O. Box 1867, Buffalo, NY. 14240-1867
> **IN CANADA:** P.O. Box 609, Fort Erie, Ontario L2A 5X3